# FALLING ON ICE

Elsa has recently fulfilled two ambitions — to open her own café, and to learn to ice skate. But her life is turned upside down when she takes part in her first competition and bumps into her teenage sweetheart, Daniel. There's still a spark between them — but is she opening herself to having her heart broken again, especially when it begins to look as if Daniel might have something to do with sinister events at the rink? Can Elsa keep her cool and prevent herself from falling on ice?

Books by Evelyn Orange
in the Linford Romance Library:

DANCE OF DANGER

# SPECIAL MESSAGE TO READERS

EVELYN ORANGE

# FALLING ON ICE

*Complete and Unabridged*

LINFORD
*Leicester*

First published in Great Britain in 2018

First Linford Edition
published 2019

A catalogue record for this book is available
from the British Library.

ISBN 978–1–4448–4006–3

Published by
F. A. Thorpe (Publishing)
Anstey, Leicestershire

Set by Words & Graphics Ltd.
Anstey, Leicestershire
Printed and bound in Great Britain by
T. J. International Ltd., Padstow, Cornwall

This book is printed on acid-free paper

*For all the amazing people*
*I met through ice skating*

.

# 1

*Why am I doing this?*

Elsa pulled her coat round her, feeling hot with nerves despite the chill of the air. The glare of the artificial lights in the ice rink made her feel faint, hardly aware of the sounds around her. It was like being cast in ice herself, her surroundings at a distance.

Applause and an echoing announcement told her that the next skater was due to perform. A tall teenage girl with dark hair twisted into a tight bun skated fiercely out onto the ice, her tiny frilled skirt bouncing as she turned neatly and raised her arm to indicate that she was ready to start. Music poured out of the loudspeakers, drowning all else as the skater began her programme. Elsa gazed in admiration at the grace and confidence the girl exuded, gliding and spinning, leaping and twirling on the glassy surface. Why, oh why had she agreed to take part in the Ice Club's annual competition?

'How are you feeling?' A woman with streaked blonde hair slipped into the seat beside her, pulling her padded coat round her. Elsa noticed that there were sparkling stickers on the woman's white skates. She smiled. Like all those who had started as adults, they had been drawn in by the lure of bling, showbiz, and TV shows.

'I feel as if my legs were about to collapse. I don't think I'll forget my programme, as I've been through it so many times. But seeing these young-sters, I wish I'd started when I was six, not twenty-six. Fiona, I don't know how you have the courage.'

Her companion laughed and joined in the round of applause that followed the end of the young skater's pro-gramme. 'I'm terrified too. It's my first competition as well. Look at me, over fifty and dressed as sparkly as a Christmas fairy! I keep telling myself not to worry, we've been skating for two years — and we've entered an appropriate class for our level.'

Elsa wished she had been skating for twenty years, right now. The next competitor was announced, and a stream of music engulfed them again. She stood up. 'I'm going to get something to drink.' Anything to prevent herself freezing solid.

It was always awkward walking on the plastic guards that protected her skate blades, so she made her way carefully past the huddle of competitors waiting to go on the ice for their warm-up session. Two coaches watched the current performance avidly, hardly heeding as Elsa squeezed through. When she pushed open the doors of the rink to go to the cafeteria, her foot slipped, and she found herself hurtling forward. Her coat went flying, and she would have joined it if a strong grip hadn't caught her.

'Steady there. You nearly came a cropper.'

Horrified by her undignified exit, Elsa stammered her thanks, looking up at the man who had arrested her fall — and froze. This was a face she had tried to forget. A long face, topped with a distinctive shock of dark hair, serious dark eyes and arched eyebrows, one raised quirkily, those shapely lips twitching in amusement at her discomfort. With a thump of her heart, she registered that he was even more attractive as a man than he had been as a teenager.

'Daniel? Daniel Whitbridge?'

His quick grin implied that he was totally relaxed at their unexpected meeting. 'Well, fancy bumping into you, Elsa. You look very glamorous — I see you've managed to tame that mane of yours.'

Her face fiery, Elsa thought how ridiculous she must look, a woman of twenty-eight in a glittering skating dress (black, admittedly) with a skirt that finished at the top of her thighs. Her hand went almost unconsciously to

4

touch her auburn curls, twisted on the back of her head and crowned with a black and silver scrunchie. Maybe she'd gone over the top a bit with the make-up, dark eyeliner and deep pink lipstick.

'I'm taking part in the competition.' Realising immediately that the explanation was totally unnecessary, she added, 'What are you doing here? I didn't think you lived in this area anymore.'

'I was having a word with Arnie, the rink manager. I haven't seen him for years.' Daniel's eyes shifted away from her, a frown touching his features briefly. He bent to retrieve her coat, and draped it round her shoulders. 'You need to keep warm.'

She shivered as the cold satin lining skimmed her bare back, with the touch of those well-remembered hands on her exposed flesh. Unwelcome memories flashed through her mind from her teenage years: Daniel kissing her before he went off to university, promising he'd invite her to stay; the long gaps between his communications that became longer as the months went by, and she tried to immerse herself in her studies to forget him; the bitter parting. No, she wouldn't let him get to her now. She tilted her face up and gave him her most defiant look.

'I heard you were married. Congratulations.'

His eyes lowered at her words. 'Not anymore. Let me buy you a drink, and I'll explain.'

*Not the best time to start reminiscing*, her head told her. 'Yes, thanks,' her mouth said. A treacherous flutter leaped inside her on discovering that he was free. She slid into a seat at the nearest table, watching him while he bought her a hot chocolate. He was wearing a thick coat, warm trousers and boots. Having been a keen skater when he was at school, Daniel was perfectly at home in this environment. His family had had the money to pay for lessons and regular sessions at the rink, whereas Elsa's mother, as the sole wage earner in the household, had only been able to afford the occasional trip.

Not long after he went to Sheffield University to study accountancy, Daniel had met Hannah, an archaeology student. Next thing Elsa had heard, they were travelling the world on archaeological digs. Then they married, moved down south, and Daniel Whitbridge dropped off the edge of her world. Three relationships later, Elsa was still single.

Daniel returned to the table and slid into the seat opposite. 'You look well, Elsa. In fact, you look great. Skating suits you.'

He seemed so at ease — could he really believe that she had forgiven him? Politeness won out. 'You haven't seen me skate yet. I've only been learning for two years, and this is my first competition.'

'So you're working locally?'

'Yes, I run the Rainbow Café on the seafront. It used to be the Copper

Kettle, but when it became available a few years ago, I took it over. Once I was doing well enough to employ some more help, I decided to join an adult class for skaters. I really enjoy it. But I didn't expect to be skating in a competition.'

His warm smile had always melted her heart, and it was doing a good job of that right now, however much she wished to resist.

'I'm sure you'll be great. Just forget about the audience, the other skaters, and perform for yourself.' He was looking at her with such intensity that it sent a tingle up her spine.

'Elsa, I . . . '

'Daddee . . . I was looking for you.' A little girl aged about six ran up and threw herself at Daniel. She was wearing a purple dress dotted with crystals, and little white skates with pink blade guards attached. Her dark hair, so like Daniel's, was plaited and pinned to her head.

'Hello, I thought you were with

Minty and her family.' He pulled her onto his knee.

'I was, but I wanted to find you. Minty's mummy said we could come and look for you.' The child looked across at Elsa with large dark eyes.

Elsa felt as if her feet were slipping from under her again. Daniel had a daughter!

'This is Poppy. Poppy, this is Elsa. We were at school together.'

Showing no interest in another adult, Poppy jumped down, taking Daniel's hand. 'Come on, there's still some skating to watch.'

Noticing another girl dressed in pink, Daniel directed Poppy towards her. 'You and Minty go back to her mummy, and I'll be with you as soon as I've drunk my coffee. Off you go, there's a good girl.'

'But Daddy . . . '

'I won't be long. Five minutes, I promise.'

Reluctantly, Poppy took her friend's hand and the pair ran off.

Elsa forced herself to speak. 'I saw her earlier in the Under Sevens. She's a natural.'

He laughed. 'Yes, she hasn't been skating long, and loves it. She was determined to enter the competition, and I thought I'd come along, revive some old memories.'

'How easy it must be to start that young. After two years, I'm still scared of falling.' As she looked into his face, she realised how apt her words were. She had fallen for Daniel once before, and had hurt herself, like on unforgiving ice. Did she really want to go through all that again? Flustered, she stood up. 'I'm due to skate soon. I'd better go.'

He followed her back through the doors, where the class before Elsa's was starting their warm-up. She shivered as the chill enveloped her once more.

'Remember what I said — perform for yourself. I'll be rooting for you.'

She gave a wry smile. 'It's not all nerves — I'm quite excited. I always wanted to do this.'

'I remember.' His eyes were kind, and she tried to stop her resolve melting. 'Let's meet up properly and talk about old times.'

'Daniel, are you sure?'

'Yes, I am. Come on, give me your number.' His jaw was set determinedly as he brought out his phone. Although she believed she would regret it, she recited her number for him. At that moment, all the skaters on the ice glided back to the gate, blades rasping as they halted and climbed on to the rubber surface. With an apologetic grin, Daniel stepped away, mouthing the words 'I'll ring' over the sparkling topknots before vanishing from her sight.

All too soon, it was Elsa's turn. As she warmed up with the other five competitors in her group, she tried to block Daniel's face from her mind, but she couldn't forget that he was out there in the darkness, watching her in the brilliance of the rink lights. Turning to execute a backward crossover, her legs nearly gave way with nerves. *No, keep skating*, she told herself. Thank goodness she would be first to compete, and didn't have any longer to wait.

'Elsa Turnfield,' the vastly amplified voice announced. She skated out and managed a creditable T-stop. Once she had struck a pose, the music began, and her feet began to move. The first spin was fine, just a little slow towards the end. Then she pushed forward, raising her back leg behind her and leaning forward into her spiral. That went well, the footwork was all right, maybe a bit stiff, and here was the jump — done! Not as high as she would have liked, but with relief she went into her final moves and returned to her opening pose. 'Thank you, Elsa,' the magnified voice intoned as she made a quick curtsey to the judges and then to the applauding audience (just a smattering in the main area, not like the huge crowds at competitions she had seen on TV, thank goodness).

'Brilliant, well done!' Fiona hissed to her at the gate, throwing her own coat on to a seat before taking to the ice.

★   ★   ★

Elsa's dreams that night were full of the competition, the ice, and Daniel smiling at her. Waking early, she was mulling over yesterday's events and trying to make sense of her disturbed feelings when her grey cat jumped on the bed, purring, padding with her dainty white paws.

'Oh, Missy, what should I do? Daniel's back, and I have to admit that he's looking good — he's free now, and wants to meet up, but he has a little girl. He might have more children, you never know. Do I really want to get involved with someone who's getting over a divorce and become a rival of a six-year-old girl?'

The cat jumped down off the duvet and ran towards the kitchen. Elsa gave up her musing and resigned herself to

13

providing breakfast for her hungry pet. Yawning, she realised that she would have to get a move on if she was to be at the ice rink in time for her class at nine o'clock. She ran her fingers through her hair, remembering with a pang how Daniel always used to tease her about her unruly curls when they were teenagers. Trust him to make a comment yesterday! In those days, she had been staunchly defiant about wearing it down to her waist in a wild tumble of waves. It was her pride, making up for having pale freckled skin. Now just beyond shoulder length, there was only time to run a wide-toothed comb through it and pull it back into a loose ponytail while she dealt with breakfast for herself and Missy.

Elsa was running late by the time she left home, her skate bag slung over her shoulder. It was too warm for tights today, so she put on a short denim skirt and stuffed her leggings into the pocket of her skate bag and a warm fleece for the rink. She would have to walk quickly to be there on time. Taking a deep breath of sea air, she drank in the view from the café round the bay, which always lifted her spirits. Today the sea was blue with just a few breakers gently washing up the smooth sand. Early dog walkers were already out.

Her friend Natalie was waiting on the corner, and waved as she approached. 'Well done, you! Fourth place in your first competition.'

'I can't believe it myself. I thought I would be last.'

'How did Fiona do?'

'Well, she did come last, but she wasn't worried because she said that she enjoyed skating her own programme. You should have done it, you know.'

Natalie wrinkled her nose. 'I know, but I just couldn't raise the courage. I was terrified when we did the Christmas show, and there were ten of us skating together! I just know that I would have fallen over.'

'You don't need to do a complicated

programme. You should have a go next time.'

'Well, maybe. I'll see how I am in the next Christmas show.'

They crossed the road and approached the ice rink.

'There seem to be a lot of cars leaving the ice rink for this time in the morning. Do you think there's been something on?' Natalie asked.

'I don't think so, not after the competition last night.' Elsa shifted her bag to her other shoulder. 'The kids were really hyper at the end. I doubt they'd be willing to get up early this morning.'

A crowd of people huddled round the entrance, parents and grandparents with children, already wearing their skates and practice dresses as they had changed at home. It wasn't until Elsa reached the door that she saw the yellow tape sealing it off. There were three skating coaches in their dark green rink coats standing outside, talking earnestly with parents. People were turned away, young girls downcast and some even in tears.

'Look, there's Fiona.' They hurried over to speak to her.

'What's going on?'

'Elsa, I can't believe it. You know Arnie Fitzsimmons, whose family own the ice rink? He's been found dead in his office.' Fiona's face was white with shock.

'*What?* When was he found?' Elsa's breath caught in her throat.

Fiona shook her head as if she still couldn't believe the news. 'Apparently it was first thing this morning. His wife called the police because he didn't return home last night. They came to the rink and found him.'

It was then that Elsa noticed the two policemen standing with the coaches outside the doors. 'Do they know what happened?'

'No one's making any sense,' Fiona said. 'You know how people talk — I even heard someone say it could be murder.'

The world around Elsa seemed to tip. Daniel had been with Arnie last night. What did he know? — and could he have had something to do with the rink owner's death?

# 2

The sky was overcast and threatening rain as Elsa slipped out early on Monday morning to buy a copy of the local newspaper from the paper shop round the corner. Resisting the urge to read it in the shop, she tucked it under her arm and hurried back home. After making herself a cup of coffee, she spread out the newspaper on the settee beside her. The story took up most of the front page.

'Ice Rink Boss Found Dead'. *'Local Ice Rink boss Arnold Fitzsimmons, 75, was found dead early this morning at the Heronsburn rink. His wife Monica, 72, contacted the police when he failed to return home after the annual club competition. Police have not stated whether his death is suspicious, but it is rumoured that Mr. Fitzsimmons was having financial problems. An inquest will be carried out next week.'*

There followed a brief history of the ice rink, built by the Fitzsimmons family in the early nineteen sixties, and the career of Arnie and his wife Monica, who were ice dance champions in their youth. It also listed the family members, sons Carl and Robert. There were three grandchildren, although their names weren't given. Elsa knew of Tara, at seventeen one of the star skaters at the rink. She had given a wonderful performance yesterday and had been awarded a cup. The two grandsons apparently played ice hockey.

At the end of the article it stated: *'Heronsburn Ice Rink will be closed for the rest of the week while police carry out their investigations.'*

Before she could dwell on it further, her land line phone rang.

'Have you seen the paper, Elsa?' Natalie's agitated voice assailed her as soon as she lifted the receiver.

'Yes, I've just finished reading it.' Elsa tucked up her legs on the settee and settled back, cradling her mug in one hand.

'I feel so sad for Monica,' Natalie continued. 'I was speaking to her last week in the shop. She's such a lovely person, always upbeat. Do you think that the rink will have to close?'

'I've no idea about the finance of such a business. The skating sessions always seem popular, and the ice hockey team is doing well.' At that moment, Missy jumped up beside her, purring as Elsa began to rub the little cat's furry cheek with one finger.

'The Heronsburn Hawks just rent the rink.'

'Surely the rink must get money from the ice hockey box office, and the refreshments. There are the university teams as well. Plus there are always lots of kids coming for ice hockey practice on a Sunday after the figure skating session ends.'

'It'll be a disaster if the rink closes. I never realised how addictive ice skating could be. And look at me, thirty five in

September.' Natalie's voice was filled with dismay.

Elsa smiled. 'Skating hooks you in, no matter what age you are. Young mums, career women, retired people — some skating twice a week, and having private lessons. It doesn't matter that we won't be skating champions — we just love it.'

At that moment, Elsa heard a ringing noise. 'I've got to go, Natalie — that's my mobile.'

'Do you want to come round tomorrow night for a meal with Mark and me?'

'That would be great. I'll be over when I'm finished at the café.'

Quickly she replaced the receiver and picked up her mobile. Her heart gave a jolt when she saw that it was an unknown number — could it be Daniel?

'Hello?' Her voice trembled, she wasn't sure why.

'Elsa? It's Daniel.'

'Hi, Daniel. Have you heard about

Arnie?' She tried to sound cool, though her heart was fluttering.

There was a momentary pause on the other end of the line before Daniel replied. 'Yes, yes I did. His son Carl contacted me on Sunday morning. It's such a shock.'

'Did Arnie seem all right when you spoke with him on Saturday?' Elsa remembered that Daniel had looked sombre when he mentioned him on Saturday.

'Yes, he was — although maybe a bit distracted. I thought it was because his granddaughter was competing, and he didn't want to miss her performance.'

'Tara's a wonderful skater. Did you watch her skate?'

'Yes, it was a superb programme. She has great talent. You did well, too.'

Elsa gave an embarrassed laugh. 'My feeble efforts are nothing to Tara's.'

'Well, you're not going to become national champion, but it was a pleasing programme. Anyway, I meant what I said about meeting up. How about a drink on Friday?'

Her heart began to pound at his invitation. She hadn't let herself believe that he was serious when he first mentioned it. Elsa had debated long with herself about whether it was right to meet, as she didn't want to revive old feelings. But they could still be friends, couldn't they? Ignoring her sensible side, she said, 'Yes, I could manage that. Are you coming up for the weekend?'

'I don't live down south anymore. I moved back to the north east three months ago, as I have some business interests here — and I wanted to be near my family.'

One of her arguments against meeting up had been the thought of a long-distance relationship. *No, stop thinking about that.* She was determined to be adult about this, and just enjoy his friendship.

So it was that she found herself sitting in a country pub a few miles from Heronsburn, waiting for Daniel to return from the bar with their drinks. Nervously, her hand smoothed the skirt of her primrose linen sleeveless dress. It was the third outfit she had put on before making her choice of what to wear. After all this time, she wanted to make a good impression on him; show him that she was grown-up and stylish, not the naïve girl he had left behind. Perhaps she should have tied her hair back, she thought as she tucked a springy curl behind one ear, hoping it didn't look too wild.

Watching him as he returned to the table carrying his pint and her wine, she felt a flip of appreciation at his trim body in jeans and dark blue shirt, sleeves rolled up to reveal tanned forearms. He'd grown from a lanky teenager into a tall, toned man. The legs beneath the denim were strong, a skater's limbs. *Don't*, she told herself firmly. She mustn't let herself be pulled back in.

'Cheers.' He touched his glass to hers, and they both took a sip of their drinks. 'I thought about you when I returned to the area, and wondered if you were still living round here. I never expected to see you at the ice rink.'

The white wine was cool on her throat. She laid the glass down on a clean cardboard beer mat. It was a new pub, with smart matching tables and light décor. 'You know how I always wanted to skate when I was younger, but money was tight.'

His face became serious. 'It was tough for your mother. How's your father?'

Elsa took a deep, ragged breath. 'He died when I was twenty-one. He developed kidney failure, and didn't manage to get a transplant in time.' Her father had been in a wheelchair since Elsa was twelve, following a motorcycling accident.

A spasm of dismay crossed Daniel's face. 'I'm so sorry; I didn't know. We really lost touch, didn't we?' He stretched out a hand to touch hers, and she grasped it, surprised at this gentleness, feeling another part of her heart melting. The boy who had been best at skating in his age group had always been a touch cocky, but the mature Daniel showed sympathy and understanding.

'What about your brother? Does he live nearby?'

She took another sip of wine. 'No. Jamie trained as a physiotherapist and works in a practice in Carlisle. He's just bought a house with his girlfriend. Is your family still living locally?'

'Yes, my parents are still in Northumberland, and my brother has a house in Heronsburn. He's married with two children. The boy, Ryan, is mad on ice hockey, and of course you met Poppy on Saturday.'

'Poppy's your *niece?* I thought she called you Daddy!'

Daniel threw back his head with a shout of laughter. 'No, she insists on calling me *Danny*, like her parents do. She had a bit of a cold on Saturday, so that's why it sounded rather nasal.' He chuckled, highly amused. 'Much as I love her, I'm glad I'm not her dad — she's quite a handful at times.'

Elsa felt as if her feet had been swept away again. He was free, living locally, and it seemed, unencumbered. Just to make sure, she asked, 'Do you and Hannah have any children?'

His expression became sober. 'No, Hannah was too dedicated to her career, and kept putting off starting a family. Two years ago when she had the opportunity to head a dig in Mexico that would take at least three years, I finally realised that she was more excited about that than she would ever be about making a family with me. We hadn't really thought things through when we got married, and just don't want the same things out of life. She was feeling the same way — we've been divorced over a year now.'

For a moment they were silent, deep in their own thoughts, letting the sounds of conversation in the pub wash round them. It was becoming more crowded, the hum of voices and laughter becoming louder.

Daniel continued, 'And what about you — is there someone special in your life?'

'Not at the moment. I've had a few relationships, but haven't found the right person yet.' Elsa didn't want him to think that she'd been sitting waiting for him to come back all these years. 'Anyway, the café takes up most of my time, plus I'm really enjoying ice skating. I'm quite content with my life.' She twisted a curl with her finger.

'Good, I'm glad to hear it.' Daniel took a long swallow of his beer. He turned as if to continue talking to her, then frowned at something that caught his eye over her head.

'What is it?' Elsa craned her neck round to see what had attracted his attention. The people in her line of vision were all strangers to her.

'I just saw Carl and Robert Fitzsimmons, and they seem to be having quite an argument.'

'Don't the brothers get along?'

Without answering her directly, Daniel continued, 'Have you heard that the ice rink is in financial trouble?'

Elsa gasped in dismay. 'So it's true?'

'Arnie was winding down, had been for several years, and he just didn't have the energy for renovation and new practices. The rink has become dilapidated, and hasn't kept up with modern trends. Skaters who made the journey from further afield now go to more modern rinks that they can reach. There's so much that needs doing — but as the rink has become less profitable, there's been even less money to go back into it.'

Daniel drained his glass and set it down on the wooden table. He rubbed his hands together as if they were cold. 'Carl's never been much of a skater, and runs the family building supplies firm. Robert was always Arnie's favourite, as he was the star of the Heronsburn Hawks in his younger years.'

'He coaches the first team now, doesn't he?'

'Yes, but he has no business sense whatsoever. Arnie was in contact with me during the past few months, with a view to me coming in as a partner in the rink. He knew that I have a few business ventures on the go that have done well. He wanted young blood. But I could see that it needed more than just me. I've been making enquiries about forming a consortium, and that was why I went to see him on Saturday. I know that Carl is in favour, but Robert thinks the rink should stay solely in the family.'

'Will it be more difficult to form a consortium, now that Arnie's gone?'

He gave a long sigh. 'I don't know. I'm meeting the family tomorrow.'

'Daniel — do you think Arnie's death had anything to do with this financial trouble? Was it suicide?'

His face set into grim lines. There was a pause before he spoke. 'I couldn't be certain, because I wasn't very close to him — but at our meeting he was positive about the proposals I was putting forward. He seemed relieved that this could save the rink, and the family's interest in it.'

Elsa suddenly felt cold. 'Well, if it wasn't suicide . . . what else could it be?'

He looked deep into her eyes. 'We'll need to wait for the results of the post-mortem, and hope that it was natural causes. Because if it wasn't, the alternative doesn't bear thinking about.'

His eyes then swivelled away, and she had a feeling that he was hiding something from her. Was there a sinister reason why he couldn't hold her gaze? Could Arnie have been *murdered?* — and could Daniel have had anything to do with it?

# 3

They talked until closing time, but didn't return to the topic of the death at the ice rink. For one brief moment, there had been a sense of horror between them, but they quickly skirted the subject and began to talk more about what they had been doing in the years since they had last met.

It seemed that Daniel had quickly tired of accountancy, though he had done all his qualifications before putting his interests into a business venture. He had helped finance a friend's computer software firm, which had reaped dividends for them both. He owned a commercial property in Newcastle that he rented to a law firm. 'It gives me a regular income, so I have the freedom to use my time for other things. I had my fingers burnt a couple of times, but I'm beginning to recognise what's likely to produce a profit. Three years ago I put money into building student flats, and I'm seeing the first profits from that now.'

'Is the ice rink going to be profitable?'

He gave a rueful smile. 'I don't know if it's my heart or my head that's leading me, but I have a strong feeling that it's my heart.'

Elsa admired the fact that as a businessman he could admit to being influenced by his emotions. But she couldn't help worrying that he was stepping into something that was clouding his judgement. 'You didn't keep on skating, did you?'

A look of sadness crossed his face. 'That's one of my serious regrets. I had been skating a long time when I went to university, and I thought I'd be able to keep it up. But somehow it lost its glamour as none of the friends I made were the least bit interested, and they saw figure skating as a bit wimpish. Stupid, I know, as it's anything but.' He laughed, but it had a bitter edge. 'I think I was too worried about my image. I was used to being the golden boy of the ice rink, and suddenly my peers were looking down on me. I wanted to do something more macho, so took up football and only went skating occasionally. Foolishly, just before my final year I had a bad accident when I was out of practice, and I wrecked my knee. I wasn't able to do big jumps anymore, and I gave up completely.'

'That must have been heart-breaking for you.'

'It was my own fault. I must say, at the time, I was more concerned about keeping my relationship with Hannah going, and I became a different person. I was rather dazzled by her — she was a stunning looker, and the brightest of her class. She wanted to do a PhD in London, and I followed her. We were married the following year, and I went into suburbia.' He shrugged his shoulders. 'So that's me.'

Elsa could see that there were a lot more layers to this man now. It wasn't the Daniel of her youth that sat before her. She wanted to know him better.

They slipped out just before closing time, squeezing through a throng of people at the door.

'Well, they say that country pubs aren't doing well, but that one's doing a roaring trade,' he commented as they walked to his car.

They made small talk during the twenty-minute drive to Elsa's café.

'You can drop me on the corner. The café is the last shop on the promenade.'

'Rubbish; I'll see you to the door. Is that it, the little shop with blue paintwork? It looks very pretty. Especially with the cat in the window up above.'

Elsa grinned. 'That's Missy. When I'm out late, she's always watching for me from the window, as if to say 'Where have you *been?*''

Elsa reached for the door handle, unsure how to make her farewells.

'Thanks, Daniel. It was a nice evening.'

'It was good to catch up. Maybe I'll see you at the ice rink sometime?'

'If it stays open, then you won't be able to keep me away. That's one of the reasons why I chose this café — it's within walking distance.'

He smiled, and inclined his head as if he was going to kiss her cheek, but then seemed to think better of it, and leaned back. 'I'll do my best to keep it going.'

Feeling a mixture of disappointment and relief that he hadn't kissed her, she opened the door and ran towards the café.

All through the weekend, Elsa kept thinking about Daniel. Scenes from their teenage relationship would flash into her mind. She'd noticed him as soon as she went to secondary school, as the school bus that picked up from the villages stopped at the end of her street to take the children into the school just up the coast. Daniel had always been tall and sure of himself, the centre of a group of athletic boys.

Although she felt disdain for their cocky antics through the years, she'd begun to admire his mop of dark hair and expressive eyes. When she'd been fourteen, he'd begun winking at her, causing her fierce embarrassment and blushes. Then after her sixteenth birthday, when he'd been seventeen, he'd asked her to come and watch him skate in the Christmas show at the ice rink.

'I can't — we don't have a car, and I can't get back home afterwards. My parents wouldn't let me take the bus that far on my own.' Miserable disappointment had wrenched at her.

'One of my friends lives near you — I'll get his dad to drop you home. We're going for a pizza after the show.'

Elsa had been enchanted by the ice rink, the costumes, the music and the skaters, and most of all, Daniel. She'd thought him a god of the ice as she'd watched him performing the most death-defying moves, it seemed. From that moment she was his willing slave, and could hardly believe that he'd chosen her. Within a few months they were seeing each other twice a week, fitting round his skating practice and their homework. Daniel passed his driving test and his parents bought him a second hand car for his eighteenth birthday, so they became even more involved. But their teenage idyll couldn't last forever.

How different for Daniel would it have been if he had stayed locally and kept on skating? Would he have become the champion that he had promised to be when he lived here? His father hadn't approved of his skating, and had pushed him to go to university. But what of herself? Could she have stayed with him as a 'groupie', admiring him and wishing she had the chance to skate too? He would probably have tired of her, and discarded her for another skating star. But that was mere speculation.

The following Tuesday morning, Elsa was laying out two large cakes she had baked when she heard the 'ting' of the café door. Looking up, she spied two elderly women entering. One had snow white hair styled into a bun, and the other a dyed blonde crop.

'There you are! I told you she'd have a carrot cake today, Dot.' The short-haired one stopped, closing her eyes and inhaling with satisfaction. 'Mmm, just smell that gorgeous coffee, too!'

'Dot and Colette! I see you've brought your skates.'

The two women took the table nearest to the counter, slinging their skating bags under their chairs. 'Two cappuccinos and two slices of that heavenly cake, Elsa, please,' Colette ordered with a smile. 'Yes, apparently they spent yesterday preparing the ice so that it could open today. Our little patch is going ahead.'

The 'patch' was the term used for a private session for regulars at the rink. Skaters had to be invited to come along, though they still had to pay. There were patches for the young figure skaters early in the morning and for students late at night, and two after school when they could have private lessons and practise away from the throng of 'fun' skaters and families that went to the general sessions. The adults had a patch on Tuesday and Friday lunchtimes, and Elsa sometimes managed to go along if she had cover in the café.

'I don't know what I'd do without the patch.' Dot pushed a loose hairpin back into her bun. 'I may not be able to jump and spin nowadays, but I can still do a good backward outside edge, and I need to keep fit. I'd like to hope that I'll still be skating at eighty, like two of our regulars.'

Elsa laid their coffees on the table. 'I'm always impressed when I see all of you over-sixties skating so well. You must make up almost half of the regular patch members.' She returned with the slices of cake, forks and serviettes.

'Ooh, this looks delicious!' Dot sliced off a piece with the fork and slid it into her mouth. 'Lovely, just the job. Are you coming today?'

'No, I can't manage today. Lisa, my assistant, is on holiday this week.'

Colette stirred a sachet of sugar into her coffee. 'Are you going to the emergency meeting of the Ice Skating Club on Friday evening?'

Busy wiping an adjoining table, Elsa paused. 'I had an email about it yesterday. Are you going?'

'No, we're not members anymore.' Dot finished off the last few crumbs of her cake. 'We'll rely on you younger ones to keep us up to date.'

Elsa arranged with Natalie that they would go to the meeting together. The skating club bar was buzzing with anticipation when they arrived. After buying drinks at the bar, they saw Fiona waving at them from across the room.

'Busy, isn't it?' she said as she pushed her way through the ever increasing crowd. 'I've never seen so many people at one of these meetings.'

Elsa scanned the throng, looking for

Daniel's familiar tall presence, but was disappointed.

'No one wants to miss out on what's going to happen to the rink,' Natalie began, but was interrupted as the doors swung open at the other end of the large room to admit a group of people. Elsa's heart gave a large thud as she saw Daniel, with Carl and Robert. To her surprise, she recognised that one of the other men was Daniel's younger brother, Andrew, but the other was unknown to her. There were also two women who followed them in.

Carl clapped his hands to draw their attention, but the conversation was already dying away at their appearance. Elsa scanned the crowd for Monica, but realised that Arnie's widow wasn't there. It must be altogether too harrowing for the elderly woman.

'Thank you for coming, everyone. I see that we have a larger attendance than normal, which makes things a bit crowded, but we'll get down to business straight away. Jean, as usual, will take the minutes.'

A woman in her fifties with short grey hair waved her hand at this mention. She was sitting on a bar stool, resting a large memo pad and pen on the bar. She was one of the staff who worked in the box office.

'You'll have heard rumours about what's going to happen to the ice rink following my father's sudden death,' Carl continued. His voice sounded tired and dispirited, which wasn't surprising. 'Arnie has had financial problems for some time, and these turned out to be worse than we realised. Dad always saw himself as the mastermind of the rink, and I'm afraid that we stood back and let him get on with it.' He glanced to his brother Robert, thinner, with longer, darker hair, at his side. Elsa noticed that he constantly glanced uneasily round the room. It made her even more curious about what would be said.

Carl continued, 'I want to put all of

your minds at rest about the future of the rink — it will be staying open, but you'll find a lot of changes, and I hope that you'll all be patient during the transitional period. Some of you may know Daniel Whitbridge, a young businessman who has been taking an interest in the ice rink. Of course he's one of our 'graduates', having been a promising figure skater in his younger years.' He turned to Daniel with an appreciative smile. 'Daniel is the head of a consortium, including his brother Andrew who is one of our ice hockey coaches, and Byron Newminster, another businessman who has done well in this region. They have bought a 50 percent holding in the rink, and Robert and I will retain the other 50 percent. Daniel and I will be joint managing directors of the ice rink, and so will be responsible for the day-to-day running of the operation. I'm now going to pass you over to Daniel, who bring you up to date about the future of the Ice Rink.'

A rumbling murmur passed round the club members as Daniel stepped forward. Elsa felt a flutter of pride as she watched him — he looked so confident, with his striking looks, his thick dark hair cresting from his forehead.

'Good evening everyone. I'm confident that this venture will be a new and exciting era for Heronsburn Ice Rink. Arnie had great vision when he built the rink in the early sixties, when he and Monica finished their ice dancing career. He dreamed of bringing ice skating to the area, for future generations. I'm sure you'll agree with me that he did.' An appreciative echo rippled through the room.

He began outlining their plans for the future: renovations, new activities, and some new building, to bring in more business and so generate new income. They also hoped to attract some big events once the building was improved.

'However, there's one matter that we've had to address at short notice, and that's the position of chief coach for the figure skating. Arnie liked to have the final say on matters in the figure skating department, so we never had an official chief coach. I'd like to introduce you to the person who'll be filling that post. We're delighted to have Irina Rostropova joining the rink as chief coach.' He turned to a tall woman with short blonde hair and a tanned face, raising his hands to begin a round of applause. Somewhat bemusedly, the spectators joined in. Elsa saw looks of utter horror on the faces of the existing Heronsburn coaches as they questioned each other. Clearly they had had no idea that this appointment was on the cards, and had been expecting one of their own number to take over that position.

Ignoring the undercurrents in the room, Daniel began to outline Irina's illustrious career, beginning in Russia and with two world championship placings, and latterly as one of the Russian Ice Star professional troupe.

He explained that she had been coaching successfully in Berkshire for the last five years.

'Irina will be bringing two of her brightest young stars to train here in Heronsburn, Bethany Pendleton and Jacob Hurwell. That in itself should raise the profile of the rink. I've known Irina for several years, and can assure you that her expertise will benefit us all.'

Irina stepped forward and gave Daniel a warm hug, kissing him on both cheeks. Her gaze lingered intimately in his eyes, and Elsa felt a stab of shock. It seemed that Daniel had brought his lover with him.

# 4

The following week, Elsa was putting two trays of muffins in the oven, apple and cinnamon, and double choc-chip. The kitchen was situated behind the main café, and was reached via a corridor that had the two customer toilets and a door that led to her tiny garden. Looking from the window as she washed her hands, Elsa could see her cat Missy prowling in the garden, a little strip at one end of her back yard. Inside, a woman's humming voice drifted down the corridor. Elsa smiled as she turned on the tap to fill the kettle. Then she called, 'Gina, are you ready for a cup of coffee?'

'Just give me a minute to finish this cubicle, and I'll be with you.'

Elsa had just placed two steaming mugs on the table when a woman in her late fifties, her dark hair pulled back into a ponytail, entered the kitchen to stow her cleaning paraphernalia in the broom cupboard by the door. After washing her hands, she sat down beside Elsa.

'Whew!' she exclaimed as she rolled her sleeves back down. 'I'm ready for this. Ta,' she added, taking a biscuit from the plate that Elsa offered. 'Mmm, ginger, my favourite. You've got a real touch with the baking, pet.'

Elsa smiled. 'I need plenty of supplies of cakes, as we're going to be busier with the holiday season starting. Are you finished for today, or do you have to work at the rink later?'

'No, it was my early shift today.' Gina also cleaned at the ice rink.

'Have you noticed any changes since the consortium took over?' Gina gave the café a good clean twice a week, but It was the first time that Elsa had really had time to talk with her in the past month, and she hadn't seen Daniel since the meeting. It had been difficult to banish the memories of their teenage years that had surfaced during the past few weeks, and she couldn't help wondering what he was doing.

'Well, those youngsters are doing a lot more late-night training. Fancy those two coming from Berkshire just to follow their coach. She must be good.'

'Tara Fitzsimmons is training with Irina Rostropova too, isn't she?'

'Yes, and I've heard that Laura, who's been her coach for many years, isn't best pleased.'

'That's a shame — Laura's my coach, too. She was a successful figure skater herself when she was younger. Didn't she come third in the British championships once?'

'My Pete always goes on about that. He was very proud that he was the one who used to grind her skates when she was a youngster. We all thought she'd be an Olympic or world champion. It was bad luck that she had an injury the year she did the championship and didn't peak at the right time.'

The buzzer on the oven went off, so Elsa jumped up to check the cakes. She took out the trays and laid them on top of the cooker. In a minute or two she would put the muffins to cool on a wire tray. She wondered how she could bring the conversation round to Daniel.

'How long has your husband been working at the ice rink?' she asked as she sat down again to finish her coffee.

'Pete was just a lad when he started out there in the sixties, when the rink opened.'

'Doesn't he find it gloomy, working in such a cold atmosphere?'

Gina laughed as she picked up the last few crumbs of her ginger biscuit with one finger, and popped them in her mouth. 'Not him! He loves it there — his own little room with his kettle and mug, and his bait box. Lots of his friends went down the mine, now *that's* a gloomy job if ever there was. He's still got his job, unlike his mining friends. He even got a place for our Sean when he left school.'

'That's your grandson, isn't it?'

'Yes. I'm pleased about that, as he's been a bit difficult growing up. I just hope that the ice rink keeps going. Poor Arnie — did you read in the paper that the inquest found sleeping pills in his system, and crushed pills were found in the glass of whisky on his desk?'

Elsa nodded. 'It was assumed that he just couldn't go on, though there was no note to say why. He's supposed to have had bad financial troubles. I'm so sorry for his wife, Monica. She's a lovely lady.'

Gina nodded. 'Well, pet, I won't keep you any longer, as you'll be wanting to open the café soon.' She nodded towards the kitchen clock, where the hands were nearing ten o'clock. 'Thanks for the coffee and the biscuit.'

'Thanks, Gina. See you on Friday.' She'd missed her opportunity to probe about Daniel, but maybe it was just as well. No doubt he was cosying up with Irina, and hearing that would just make her feel miserable.

To her relief, the next few days were too busy for thoughts of her former teenage boyfriend to intrude. The local primary school was having its summer fete, and Elsa had volunteered to judge a baking competition, as well as provide dozens of cupcakes for the afternoon teas. It had been fun designing them in different colours. Each had a coloured frosting in pink, blue and yellow, and she had used edible paints to design flat icing discs in shapes of seashells, starfish, anchors and yachts to put on the top of each one. Katy, a student who worked at weekends, had come in on the Friday evening to help her decorate them. On the Saturday, Katy's boyfriend, Tom, brought his car at noon to convey the two of them plus the boxes of finished baking to the school. Lisa was holding the fort at the café.

★　★　★

Once they had delivered the cakes, Katy went back to help Lisa, and Elsa had a look round before she was needed for the cake competition. Heronsburn Primary School had done itself proud this year. There were many colourful stalls, including a tombola, bean bag tossing, a water pistol tincan alley, and 'guess how many sweets in a jar'. This year's star attraction was a large bouncy castle, already wobbling with the efforts of many enthusiastic children. Beside this there was a large poster showing times of the competitions — races for all ages later in the day, and the cake competition that Elsa was due to judge, at three o'clock.

The tombola stall was doing well, run by a balding man wearing a green T-shirt that barely hid his ample belly, printed with 'Heronsburn Primary PTA' in black lettering. He had a booming voice and a ready laugh. There was a loud cheer just as Elsa approached.

'Well done to Mrs. Jenkins! The proud winner of a cool box, donated by our local freezer shop!'

The delighted mother held aloft her prize, clapped enthusiastically by the small crowd round the stall. As Elsa was watching, two large hands came over her eyes, and a deep voice murmured 'Surprise!' in her ear.

Removing the hands and whirling round, Elsa found herself looking into Daniel's grinning face. Her heart, already hammering in surprise, seemed to skip a beat. He'd been hovering on the edges of her thoughts for days, and it was as if she'd conjured up his presence.

'What are you doing here?' she gasped.

His eyes crinkled at the corners as his lips curved. 'Just getting back into the neighbourhood — and supporting my family.' His arm snaked round the shoulders of a young woman standing beside him. Her long dark blonde hair cascaded over his hand as he hugged her firmly. 'This is my sister-in-law, Vicki. My niece and nephew are pupils at Heronsburn Primary.'

Elsa tried to compose herself so that she wouldn't look like the gauche teenager who had surfaced within her. 'Nice to meet you, Vicki. I'm Elsa. I used to know Daniel at school.'

A dimple appeared in Vicki's cheek as her smile deepened. 'And very well, too, I understand. Good to meet you at last, Elsa.'

Her cheeks flaming, Elsa wondered what Daniel had told Vicki about her. 'Where are the kids? I've been in the refreshment tent, delivering my cupcakes.'

He grinned. 'Ryan and his friends are manning the water-pistol shooting range. I just hope they're not soaked before the end of their hour stint.'

Vicki chuckled. 'I've got some spare clothes in the car, just in case. Andrew's overseeing Poppy on the bouncy castle. I insisted that she go on it before eating, as we don't want to see her lunch reappearing.'

Elsa laughed, warming to Daniel's sister-in-law with her relaxed manner.

'Have you entered for the cake competition? I'm to judge it later.'

With a snort of laughter, she replied, 'No way. I can just about manage cupcakes for a treat, but I just don't have time to bake. I work as a teaching assistant, and then it's full-on when Ryan and Poppy are around. Andrew works for a chain of sports shops when he's not playing ice hockey. I'll enjoy having some cake here today.'

'So will I,' Daniel chipped in. 'I haven't had the chance to visit your café, but I hear good things about your baking. I think I'll go straight to the refreshment tent now, so I don't miss out.' His gaze seemed to intensify. 'Would you like something? How about an ice cream?'

'Thanks, but it's nearly closing time for the cake competition, so I'd better head over there.' A shaft of disappointment caught her at having to part company. Elsa drank in the sight of Daniel's long muscular body as he strolled towards the bouncy castle with

Vicki. Reluctantly, she tore her eyes away and went on her way.

The cake competition was being held in a small portable classroom in the school yard, where all was safe from prying eyes and insects until the entries had been tasted and judged. There were seventeen entries, all of which looked inviting.

Elsa began slicing slivers from each cake and examining the textures carefully before sampling a taste. There were some very imaginative creations, including a train, a butterfly and a flower pot complete with flowers. In the end she was torn between two excellent entries, one an orange cake fashioned to look like a football, the other an unusual sponge with cream-cheese frosting dusted over with toasted cake crumbs. In the end she decided to award the prize to the more unusual cake, as the flavour and texture impressed her.

The deputy head, Mr Mayhew, announced over the loudspeaker that the results of the cake competition were ready. Elsa was surprised at how many people crowded into the little class-room. Her eyes were immediately drawn to Daniel with Vicki, standing near the front. His eye closed in a slow wink, setting up a fluttering in her chest which she tried to ignore. Was he trying deliberately to fluster her, reminding her of being a teenager?

Mr. Mayhew thanked everyone for coming to the fete. 'I'm delighted to introduce you to Elsa Turnfield, the judge for our cake competition. If you haven't tasted the delights of her Rainbow Café on our seafront, then you've missed a treat. So what better person to assess the efforts of our local bakers, someone who's a true profes-sional. I'm looking forward to hearing her views. Please welcome Elsa!'

Applause rang in Elsa's ears as she stepped up on to the small platform beside Mr. Mayhew, and to her astonishment someone whistled. Some-how she knew that it was Daniel, who was standing with Vicki, applauding enthusiastically. Conscious of his presence with every word she spoke, she congratulated all the entrants for the high standard of baking.

'I know everyone's dying to know who the winner is, so I won't waste time. The runner-up created a true delight for the taste buds, a zingy orange cake with a light, springy texture, and the added novelty of a sporting design.' Before she announced the identity, a woman at the back had already recognised the description of her cake and emitted a squeal of delight. 'Number six!'

A woman in her sixties pushed her way through the crowd, a beam of sheer happiness on her face, closely followed by two little boys who shouted, 'Yay, that's our gran!'

Elsa found herself enveloped in a warm hug and a waft of floral perfume as the woman took her certificate, holding it aloft as everyone applauded and the little boys' mother took several photos.

Finally they all calmed down, and Elsa, grinning, was able to announce the winner. 'And now, what you've all been waiting for. All the entries this year were superb, but one stood out for me, principally because it was so unusual. A light-textured two-tone sponge with the most delicious cream-cheese frosting, and the unusual topping of toasted cake crumbs, bringing together a real symphony of textures and flavours. So I am very pleased to announce that the champion cake baker of Heronsburn this year is baker number eleven!'

Applause rang out as everyone looked round to find out the identity of the winner. The crowd parted and a tall woman with short blonde hair made her way through, smiling broadly. Elsa's eyes widened. It was Irina! What was she doing here?

She climbed up on to the platform and stood beside Elsa, who bemusedly handed over the winner's certificate and rosette. Irina gave her a quick hug, but her eyes showed no recognition as she took her prize. However, she turned to the people applauding her victory.

'Thank you so much,' she told them, her voice deeply sexy and tinged with a strong Russian accent. 'This was my grandmother's recipe, a Russian favourite called *biskvit*.' She turned back to Elsa. 'She was a magnificent cook. It shows real discernment to recognise this. Thank you.'

Taken aback, Elsa could only stammer, 'It was so unusual — and delicious.'

Mr. Mayhew then told the crowd that they would be able to buy portions of the cakes in half an hour. They began to disperse, and Elsa searched for Daniel and Vicki. She was met with the sight of him embracing Irina, smiling intimately into her eyes. A physical pain shot through Elsa's body, making her draw in her breath sharply. Unable to look at them any longer, she turned on her heel and went to the cakes to begin portioning them out for the sale. Her hands were shaking, and she had to take a few deep breaths before starting the task with the sharp knife. As the minutes passed and the room cleared she became calmer, but her thoughts were still disturbed. She said goodbye to the Mayhews and headed for the refreshment tent to see if she was needed.

All the cupcakes had been sold, so there was nothing to collect. Elsa began to walk back to the café, the events of the day swirling round her mind. The look that had passed between Irina and Daniel when he was congratulating her repeated like an action replay on television, squeezing her foolish heart with every thought. It was a relief to reach the café at last and discover that there were tables to clear and a stack of dishes to unload from the dishwasher. Elsa plunged into work gratefully.

# 5

Slipping into the rink for an early session on Friday morning, Elsa noticed that there was a brand new photo of Irina in the centre of the display board at the ice rink. None of the other coaches had the exotic mystery of the new Russian coach with her heavy eye make-up and red lipstick.

Jean smiled at her as she took Elsa's money. 'Last quiet session before the schools break up tomorrow.'

'I made a point of coming — the next six weeks will be overflowing with kids, especially if the weather's bad.'

'That's the problem with a seaside resort. We don't want sunny weather, otherwise they'll all desert us for the beach!'

Elsa was chuckling to herself as she hurried through the nearest door to put her skates on. She almost bumped into Irina who was coming the opposite way. The Russian always wore figure-hugging outfits, and didn't sport the regulation heavy warm green coat printed with 'Heronsburn Ice Rink Coach'. Her jacket was trimmed with very realistic fur, as was her hat.

Elsa was about to greet her when Irina swept past without a glance. Elsa turned and looked after her indignantly before stumping up the stairs, and flipped down one of the plastic rinkside seats so that she could put on her skates. Irina clearly couldn't even be bothered to remember that Elsa had presented her with a prize for her cake. It was as if the coach perceived an adult recreational skater as being beneath her notice. It was especially galling as Elsa had decided to be mature about the situation with Daniel and gracious in defeat!

Once Elsa was skating with long steady strokes round the empty ice, her pique evaporated, and she began to let the rhythm and movement take her over. It was always relaxing to go through her warm up routine, doing various simple moves and getting used to the edges of her skates again. Soon she didn't notice the cold as her blood began to circulate faster.

After about ten minutes, no one else had arrived, so she decided to work on her competition programme. As she went over her moves, she was aware that a young couple wearing hire skates had come on to the ice, and an older woman wearing her own skates began to practise. Elsa was lost in her own world, concentrating on her pro-gramme. Then she made an effort to go faster on her backward crossovers before entering the spin, and felt her blades catch with a loud 'click'. Staggering, she managed to regain her balance, at the same time finding her arm caught in a strong grip. Heart pounding at the near fall, she turned to thank her saviour, and gasped.

'Daniel!' How long had he been on

the ice? Had he been watching her?

'Hello, Elsa. Why did you dash off the other day after the cake competition? I was looking for you, but you'd gone already.' He was wearing a black fleece and trousers, and a red scarf peeped out from beneath his collar. His hair was uncovered, springing up wildly.

*I didn't want to see you and Irina being all lovey-dovey*, she wanted to say. Instead she told him, 'I had to get back to the café. Saturday is our busiest day.'

He nodded, then continued, 'I'm impressed with how much your skating has improved since the competition.'

'Well, that wouldn't be difficult,' she retorted, 'seeing as I was so nervous that day. I can skate the routine much better.'

He grinned, and she felt the treacherous flip inside her. She wished fiercely that she didn't react that way to him. He was the boy who had broken her heart and was now involved with another woman.

'I'm sure you can,' he said. 'Are you in Laura's group?'

'Yes, she's a really good coach. We're going to start polishing my programme again so that I'll be ready for the autumn quarterly skating club competition.'

'Good. Do you think there's a lot of enthusiasm amongst the adults for the competitions? Arnie wanted to encourage more adult participation in competitions, and I feel that it would be a good route to follow. It was never like that when I was at school.'

'Television has a lot to answer for.'

He laughed. 'I'm glad that reality shows have become so popular. Would you like to skate round with me?' He held out his hand. Mesmerised by his presence, Elsa could only stretch out her arm to put her own gloved hand in his. As they began to glide over the ice together, she recalled that she had dreamed of skating with him as a teenager, and here they were twelve years later actually doing this. Despite wearing gloves, the touch of his hand still seemed to send a bolt of electricity up her arm.

Suddenly her toe pick caught in a groove on the ice, and she gave a clumsy stagger forward. Furious with herself, she felt her pale skin warm with embarrassment. Pretending that nothing had happened, she made herself concentrate on her skating and not be distracted by his touch or his expertise.

After a couple of times round the rink, she began to relax and enjoy the experience. They were skating faster than she had ever done before, and the sensation of the icy air racing past her was exhilarating. She began to laugh with delight when he took both her hands, and pushed her backwards round the rink at great speed. Circuit after circuit, the rasp of the blades on their boots accompanied the rink music. Finally he put his arms round her waist and they did a double turn to come to a halt.

His grin was wider than she had ever

seen before. 'If you can get more speed like that, it'll really improve your performance. How did it feel?'

'Wonderful!' she laughed. 'But it's so much easier when you're holding me.' Then she realised what she had said, and gasped.

Daniel didn't seem to have noticed the double meaning to her words, just nodding in agreement. 'Now you've had the sensation of going faster, you'll feel better doing it on your own.' He looked up at the clock. 'I'm afraid my free time is over. I've a meeting upstairs at half past eleven. I'd better take my skates off and look respectable.'

Disappointment washed over Elsa. It had been so exciting skating with him. Even more gratifyingly, he wasn't condescending and seemed genuinely pleased with her progress.

There was a chiming noise from his pocket. Whipping off his glove, he took out his phone and touched the screen. 'Irina's waiting for me — I'd better go. Enjoy your practice.' So saying, he skated to the gate and stepped out on to the rubber rinkside surface.

All Elsa's exhilaration evaporated. He was going to see Irina — she was relegated to the status of an old friend. Her practice ruined, she skated round a few more times before removing her skates and dragging her feet back home.

Elsa tossed and turned that night, waking frequently and at one point lying awake for at least an hour. No matter how much she told herself that it was foolish to let her emotions be engaged once more, that their relationship had ended when Daniel went to university, she couldn't deny that her feelings for him had been stirred up in the past few weeks.

Her attempts to sleep weren't helped by a loud noise from the side street in the early hours. Unable to relax, she got out of bed and looked through a crack in the curtains, to see a huge lorry reversing into the side street that the window overlooked. It was a monster of a truck, and only just missed her neighbour's car. Then it pulled out again and went off in the direction of the ice rink. As she stepped back into bed, Elsa could see on her bedside clock that it was just past three thirty.

She eventually sank into slumber once it had become light, and woke with a start when her alarm clock sounded at seven o'clock. She had the weekend baking to do, and would be opening at ten o'clock as usual. Once Lisa arrived, she would begin to make the Saturday lunch sandwiches and salads that were always on the menu.

For the first time ever, the café felt like a millstone to Elsa. She wished that she could just go away somewhere for a few days to clear her mind and banish the unwelcome feelings for Daniel that were surfacing. Luckily it was a busy day, which helped to keep her mind occupied. At half past one, Natalie breezed into the café with her husband, Mark. While he sat down at the only vacant table, she came straight up to the counter, and pounced once Elsa had given change to a customer.

'Zach has invited us all to go out for a drink tonight, as he's just had promotion in his job. We said that we'd call for you. Will 8.30 be all right?'

Elsa blinked and shook her head in disbelief. 'And what if I already have an arrangement? I can't just drop everything for your brother, can I?'

Natalie gave a smirk. 'But you don't, do you?' Then her gaze came to rest on the counter. 'Oh, good, you've still got some chicken salad left. I'll have one of those, and Mark will have a prawn and avocado sandwich. Plus an Americano and a latte, please.'

Elsa threw up her hands in mock dismay. 'Patience, patience! I'm very busy today, madam, but will attend to your order as soon as I can. Now shoo, go and sit down.' An elderly couple came up to pay their bill, so Natalie complied.

Lisa took over their orders, while Elsa served up some cake for another customer and brought coffee refills to another table. Thankfully, Katy came back from her lunch break and began cleaning tables. Elsa hadn't a moment to think, but eventually the café cleared except for two women having tea and cake in the corner. Lisa started wiping down the counter, while Katy took the dishes through to the kitchen.

Natalie caught Elsa's eye and waved her over. Mark dragged a chair from the next table so that she could sit down.

Elsa had a tray in her hands. 'I really should clear those tables, as it looks as if everyone's out and about today. The afternoon tea slot is going to start early.'

'Nonsense; you've got to have ten minutes off your feet. Now, about tonight . . . '

'I really don't think I'm going to have the energy for a night out.'

Mark, usually quiet beside his wife's bubbly enthusiasm, chipped in. 'Don't worry, we're not planning on staying that late. After all, you both have to get up early for your skating class tomorrow.'

Elsa laughed. 'That hasn't stopped Natalie in the past. You came to the class after a Christmas party last year, and you'd been up until three o'clock!'

'I was still running on adrenalin!' Natalie giggled. 'Though I must admit, I did fall over when I did my backward crossovers. But I'm much better at skating now. Still, if Zach wants to go on to a nightclub, he'll just have to take his other friends.'

Elsa gave in, realising that she'd have to get herself out of her rut, and Zach could be fun, if only she could let herself go. But her chat with Natalie was cut short as the café door swung open, bringing more customers. Soon she was embroiled in orders, and could only wave and nod at Mark and Natalie who called 'Eight thirty!' on her way out.

That evening, the pub was already busy when the three of them arrived. A long-limbed young man with light brown hair waved from a table near the bar. There was another couple sitting with him.

'Great — Zach's already bagged a table, and that's Paul and Nell with him. You know them; they work in the same office.'

'I met them at his party in the spring,' Elsa said as she slipped off her denim jacket. She had chosen a sleeveless white cotton blouse and red skinny jeans for the evening. These days she didn't worry that the red clashed with her hair, which she had left loose and curly.

Mark went for the drinks while the two young women sat down.

'Nat! Els! Great to see you. Shuffle up, you two. There's a stool for Mark you can pinch from the next table.'

'I wish you wouldn't always shorten people's names to one syllable,' Elsa grumbled.

'If you had been christened Zachary, then you would agree that short names are best.' His ready smile won her over, and soon he had them in stitches with his impersonations of some of his colleagues. He worked in the payroll department at the local council offices, while his sister was an assistant in the education department. Mark was a geography teacher at the local comprehensive school.

Later in the evening, Elsa found herself sitting next to Zach, taking a crisp from the packet that he was offering her. 'I've decided to go for it,' he said. 'I'm coming along to the adult ice skating classes tomorrow.'

Elsa's crisp remained poised before her open mouth. 'Never! You'd better bring a cushion, then, because the last time you went skating with us, you spent more time on your backside than upright.'

He grinned sheepishly. 'Well, I thought that the coach might make a better job of teaching me than you two did. Anyway, Nat says that I have to be committed to it if I want to impress you.'

Elsa nearly choked on her crisp. '*Impress me?* Zach, you're not serious!'

All at once his face was sober. 'I mean it, Els. I've always liked you, but I don't want you to just see me as Nat's goofy little brother. Anyway,' he added with a flicker of a smile, I am actually older than you.'

'You might act it, then!' she retorted, then giggled. After the long day and bad night's sleep, the wine was going to her head. Taking a good long look at Zach, she had to admit that he was quite presentable. Maybe it was time that she accepted that Daniel was nothing more than her teenage ex. 'I challenge you to stay upright for more than five minutes tomorrow.'

He laughed. 'Accepted! If I do, you're buying me a drink.'

Next morning, Elsa and Natalie tried to concentrate on their lesson with Zach watching from the side. By the end of the half hour, they were both hot and bothered despite the chill temperature, trying to learn a new jump. As they headed for the gate, Zach was waiting with his hire skates on, towering over the group of women clustering at the gate to come on the ice for the elementary classes.

The adult beginners' group had the area of ice nearest the entrance. Natalie and Elsa watched Zach as he lurched backwards and forwards across the ice, but had to admit that he was soon finding his confidence. He quickly abandoned the helping hand of the coach, and was trying to skate properly. 'Laura's great with adult beginners,' Natalie commented. 'She had me skating properly on the first day as well.'

'Me too,' Elsa said. 'It's not quite the same, going skating with your friends in hire skates. I couldn't believe how much I achieved in my first lesson.'

'But you're a natural.'

'Maybe I would have been if I had started when I was a child. Still, I'm amazed at how much I've learned in a short time.'

By the time Zach came off the ice, grinning widely, his hair was standing on end with effort. 'You see, I did it! You owe me that drink, Els!'

'Hot chocolate?' Her face was mischievous.

'Something a bit stronger, I think. I only fell over twice.'

Natalie shoved up so that he could sit next to them. 'Get those skates off. You've to go straight into the shop and buy a pair of your own, if you're going to do it properly. Hire skates are useless.'

The shop had reopened the previous week, and had been crowded during opening hours with people desperate for new skating clothes and equipment. When the three friends entered, Monica was busy ringing up a payment. Two teenage girls were looking through the leggings, and a father was with his son trying out an ice hockey stick.

The shop was tiny, with boxes of ice skates lining a high shelf all the way round. On one wall there was a display of skates of various kinds.

'I'm not spending a lot, mind,' Zach stated. 'I may never get past the stage I'm at right now.'

'Don't be so faint-hearted,' his sister said, fingering a display of practice tops. 'You'll improve every week, as long as you practise as well.'

Monica approached them with a smile. 'Now, what can I help you with?'

'My brother has just started lessons, and needs skates of his own.'

Elsa thought that Monica looked thinner and rather drawn. It wasn't surprising, after what she had gone through. Once Monica had given Zach some tips about lacing his boots and he was walking round the shop, Elsa said, 'It's nice to see you again, Monica. We've missed you.'

The elderly woman gave a pinched smile. 'It's good to be back. At first I thought I couldn't face coming in to the rink after what happened.' She took a deep breath. 'Then I realised that I needed the shop and the company. I love seeing all the little ones and the enthusiasm on their faces. The little girls just light up when they see the sparkle and frills. And the ice hockey boys are so excited when they imagine themselves playing like their heroes. Daniel's talking about getting me a permanent assistant, rather than just one of the box office girls to fill in.'

'He's really pushing the boat out, isn't he?' Elsa wondered where he would be finding the money for another member of staff.

'Yes, there are going to be renovations starting soon. The only thing that bothers me,' she added, frowning, 'is that he wants to begin an internet service for the shop. If we start making money from that, then he's going to bring in the assistant. How I'm going to manage it myself, I don't know.'

At that moment, Zach returned, declaring himself satisfied with the skates.

'Why not have a go on the ice with

them now?' Monica suggested. 'The public skating session is under way. I'll look after your stuff here if you like.'

'Good idea. Come on, Zach.' Once he had paid for his skates, Natalie took him straight back into the ice rink.

Elsa held back, telling Natalie and Zach that she wanted to look for some practice clothes. Once they had gone she returned to Monica, who was laying out some items in the display case below the counter. 'Do you think Daniel would mind if I help you out with the internet orders? The café's closed on Mondays, so I could pop along for a couple of hours in the morning and do some legwork for you. I'm quite happy with computers.' It would be fun to be involved behind the scenes at the ice rink, and she wanted to make things easier for Monica. 'When would it start?'

Monica's face lit up. 'Sometime in September. Daniel has asked me to think of a few new lines and possibly some additional suppliers. He's even talking of extending the shop so that there's more storage. Maybe we'll even get a little changing room.' She smiled.

At that instant the door flung open, and a tall young woman with blonde hair twisted into a bun breezed into the shop. She had dark eyes made up with eyeliner, and smooth, flawless skin, but the lips that were coloured with pale pink lipstick were drawn into a sulky pout. 'At last! I came earlier but you weren't here.' She wheeled her trolley skate case in through the door and plumped it down in front of Monica. 'I need four pairs of beige tights, two of them with crystals. Can you get them out for me while I take a look at your practice clothes?'

Both Elsa and Monica looked on in bewilderment as the young woman sauntered over to the racks and began to rifle through the skating tops. A look passed between them, and Monica mouthed the word, *Bethany*. Elsa nodded. So this was the new 'superstar' that Irina had brought with her to the area. Elsa pretended to examine the leg warmers piled up on the counter, and Monica began to look out the tights. It wouldn't do to carry on their conversation in the presence of this stranger.

Within a few minutes, Bethany was back at the counter, her eyes contemptuous. 'You haven't anything decent in my size. It's all little girl stuff. I must say, I thought that the shop would be better stocked. I'll just have to get something off the internet.'

'Well, we're waiting for an order coming from Canada, so if you come back in a couple of weeks it should have arrived by then. If there's something you particularly want, I can add it to the order I'm placing at the end of September.'

'No, thanks. I can't wait that long. How much are these?' She pointed a long purple-lacquered fingernail at the four packets of tights. Monica told her, but added that she couldn't take the credit card payment in the shop. 'I'll do the bill, and you need to pay at the box office.'

With an exaggerated sigh of frustration, Bethany almost snatched the bill from Monica's fingers and stalked out.

'Well!' Elsa couldn't think of anything else to say.

'I've heard a lot about her, but that's the first time I've met Bethany. Our Tara said that she'd been quite nasty to her about her skating. We're not used to unpleasantness like that at this ice rink. Maybe it's normal where she comes from.' Monica pulled out a small plastic carrier bag and put the tights in it.

'Poor Tara. She's a lovely skater, and it's rotten if someone tries to knock your confidence. Everyone is so kind to me, and I'm not very good.'

The door swung open and Bethany slapped the receipt on the counter. Without another word, she took the bag from Monica's outstretched hand. Then she picked up the handle of her skate trolley and swept out of the shop.

'I'll be very glad if she gets *all* of her

stuff online. The less I see of her, the better.' Monica rang open the till and put the receipt in the tray.

Elsa rejoined the others on the ice. After another hour, Zach declared himself totally exhausted, especially as the session had become very busy with families.

'Well done — you'll soon be doing jumps and spins,' Elsa laughed as they returned to the shop to pick up his shoes.

Outside the door, Zach suddenly grabbed her and twirled her round, lifted her off her feet and slung her over his shoulder. 'How about an ice dancing partnership?'

'Let me go, you goon!'

He put Elsa on her feet, but enveloped her in a great bear hug and planted a kiss on her lips. 'Forfeit!'

She gave him a push, laughing. 'It'll be a long time before I trust you to do that on the ice!' Then she looked up, and saw Daniel entering the main door of the ice rink. From the look of surprise on his face, he must have witnessed everything that had gone on, and she felt her cheeks grow hot. What idiots they must have looked, grown adults clowning around.

Then someone called Daniel's name and caught his attention. Before she followed Natalie and Zach into the shop, Elsa risked another glance at him. Their eyes met, and he raised his eyebrows, unsmiling. She whirled round and away, angry with herself. She was certain that little bit of harmless fun had made her look a fool in Daniel's eyes.

# 6

Daniel didn't come to the café, or even try ringing for a chat. Elsa surmised that either he was truly disgusted at her childish behaviour, or thought that there was something going on between her and Zach. Well, she wasn't going to ring him either — he might be with Irina.

On the first Monday morning in September, Elsa went to help Monica in the shop as she had promised. The unique smell of the rink leached out into the surrounding air as she reached the door. She had never worked out what it was — probably the rubber matting, or a damp smell from the old felt that carpeted the foyer. The public session wouldn't start for another fifteen minutes, so she had to knock on the locked door to attract the attention of someone manning the box office.

Jean, wrapped up warmly in a fleece and scarf, came to the door. 'You're keen this morning, Elsa.'

'I'm not here to skate — I volunteered to help Monica start the online shop until there's a permanent assistant.' The hallway was cooler than the September morning outside.

There was a light on in the shop, illuminating Monica hanging up some girls' dresses on a rack. When Elsa opened the door, Monica beamed at her. 'I've only just arrived myself. Our order has come, so I was unpacking it. Would you like to help me price items and hang them up, and that would get you used to where the stock is kept?'

Elsa agreed, stowing her shoulder bag behind the counter. There were two large cardboard boxes on the floor with clothing packed in clear plastic bags. Monica pulled the blind down on the glass door, making sure that the 'closed' sign was clearly visible on the other side. 'There won't be many skaters this morning as the children are all back at school. There might be the odd student, otherwise I expect it'll be a usual quiet Monday morning.'

Elsa and Monica spent the next hour putting clothing on hangers. 'Aren't these gorgeous!' was the frequent exclamation as she took packages out of the box — dresses in rainbow colours, some in warm lined velvet, others with sparkling patterns, then leggings encrusted with crystals outlining images of ice skates or skaters. There were Lycra flounced skirts in bright neon colours, and others in graceful georgette. Most of the items were in children's sizes, some quite tiny, as the little girls started as young as three.

Monica stretched her arms and reached for a battered old vacuum flask. 'Have you brought a drink with you?'

'No, I'll go along to the vending machines. I won't be long.'

Jean waved at her from the box office. 'Only a few skaters in,' she called as she tapped on the keyboard of the office computer. Elsa was almost wishing she had brought her skates, for there was nothing she liked more than to skate on a quiet rink. But the shop was her priority today.

The corridor was dark and eerily silent as she pushed open the doors of the rink café. This really wasn't much more than a hatch, shuttered now, and the empty benches starkly utilitarian. From beyond the far door reached the drone of grinding metal, where one of the maintenance team was sharpening skate blades. There was a constant row of skates waiting to be dealt with each week. Constant practice made the blades blunt and likely to skid on the ice. Elsa wondered if it was Pete, her cleaner's husband, who was working today.

The vending machines were in the next corridor, next to the skate hire. Opening the door, she found that the light was off, and it took her a moment to locate the switch with her fingers. Her heart leaped in fright as there was a scuffling and banging noise directly in front of her. The light came on and flooded the area. Two young men and an older one were sitting on the long wooden blocks that served as seating for people putting on their skates. They regarded her with surly expressions.

A flicker of apprehension touched Elsa at the hostility in their faces. The sound of grinding continued from beyond. These must be maintenance staff, she thought, but what they had been doing in the dark, she couldn't imagine. 'Oh, hi,' she said brightly. 'I'm sorry to disturb you. I'm just going for a drink.' She waved towards the vending machines along the corridor, and hurried past. Her hands were shaking as she fumbled in her purse for some coins. She felt relieved when the plastic bottle thudded into the dispensing well, and she grabbed it quickly.

The three men hadn't moved from the benches, their eyes following her as she walked past. The entrance foyer with Jean and Monica's presence was a welcome haven. She couldn't tell why she felt that the encounter was sinister, and it seemed less significant when she told Monica, who shrugged her shoulders.

'Well, I'm not sure what's going on these days, pet. There are new staff wandering round, men who I never knew in my Arnie's day. And of course, there are renovations starting. Those men might just be builders looking over the place. My son Carl was telling me that the whole of the inside is to be painted, starting soon, plus repairs to the seating. He's using some of his contacts from the building trade. The extension to the shop is starting next week. That's why I wanted to get this online business started. Daniel said he'd come in to show you what to do.'

Her heart gave a huge lurch. Daniel! She hadn't expected that. Almost at the sound of his name, he appeared in the doorway. 'Hello, Monica. Elsa — good of you to come. The shop's looking great. I'm sure the kids will flock in this week to see the new stock.'

'I've never seen it looking so attractive.' Elsa tried to speak casually, though her pulses were racing.

'Yes, we're starting a kid's competition at the end of October, to encourage the youngsters who aren't ready to compete in a club competition.'

'And we'll sell a lot more outfits because they'll all want to look pretty,' Monica added with a little smile.

Daniel gave his attractive grin and rolled up the sleeves of his sweatshirt. 'Now, let's get this computer up and running.'

The brand new computer had been set up in a corner of the shop's backroom. Daniel showed her how they would pick up the orders. 'Oh, good, there are already one or two. The computer guy set it all up last week, but you'll also need to start inputting the new stock from the delivery notes.' He turned and looked at her, which made her breath feel short. 'I really do appreciate you doing this, Elsa. I know how busy you are with your own business.' He brushed his hand over her shoulder, which made her shiver with half-forgotten pleasure.

She turned to look at the computer screen, hoping that her jitters didn't show. 'Well, hopefully it won't take me long to get used to it, and then I can just pop in a couple of times a week to do the computer stuff.' How did her voice sound so calm?

'I picked up some packaging at the wholesale shop, but I advise you to start ordering it online. We'll arrange to set up a business account. It would be great if you could monitor the traffic we get through the online ordering, and adjust the website accordingly.'

He made sure that she was familiar with the necessary passwords. Feeling his warm breath on her cheek, Elsa had to work hard concentrating on his instructions.

Finally Daniel leaned back. 'I have to go. Carl and I are expecting some industrial decorators soon to discuss the colour scheme for the new paint-work.' He squeezed her shoulder, then released it abruptly, stepping back. Their eyes met again. 'Elsa . . . '

He paused and frowned, and she held her breath in anticipation of what he was going to say. But finally he said, 'Let me know if you have any problems.'

'Thanks, Daniel.' Reluctantly, Elsa forced herself to turn away and began listing the items that needed to be dispatched.

'I'll see you soon,' he said.

She turned her head, but he had disappeared. All at once the spark had gone from her day. Sighing, she returned to her task, reminding herself that she had to forget him, as he belonged to someone else. How gullible she was, to begin falling for him again for no reason.

The following Sunday, Elsa was waiting for a bus to take her to Morpeth, the Northumberland market town where her mother lived. A miserable drizzle had set in, so she huddled in the shelter, hoping that the bus would be on time.

She began wondering whether she should encourage Zach, who still liked her. They always had a good laugh together. Whereas Daniel made her feel disturbed. Surely it was better to be comfortable with someone than to be on edge?

Suddenly a voice intruded on her thoughts. 'Elsa! Can I give you a lift somewhere?'

With a jolt, she realised that it was Daniel calling through the open window of his car. She had been so wrapped up in her thoughts that she hadn't noticed it pull up at the kerb.

The familiar twist of excitement caught her. 'I'm visiting my mother in Morpeth.'

He leaned over to open the door. 'Then jump in — I'm off to see my parents as well, so I'm going in that direction.'

Relief mingled with pleasure as she accepted his invitation. She hadn't fancied the bus ride through the rain, and then the half-mile walk at the other end.

Once they had joined the other traffic, Daniel asked, 'Has your mother lived there long?'

'Since Dad died. She moved from the village to be nearer her work, and there are more activities for her nearby.'

'That sounds ideal. I remember her being a sociable person. But it's not much fun going by bus on such a grim day.'

Elsa shrugged. 'I can't afford a car at present. But today's important — my mum's been talking about her new man for a while, and she wants me to meet him.'

'I see. And how do you feel about that?'

She rubbed her face self-consciously. 'She's had dates before in the past few years, but this is the first time she's asked me to meet anyone. He must be special.'

'Does that worry you?'

Elsa sighed. 'I'm prepared to be open-minded.' Even to her, this didn't sound convincing.

'Of course.' Their conversation dwindled for a few minutes while Daniel negotiated a busy roundabout.

Once they were on the dual carriageway, Elsa decided to change the subject. 'How are you getting on at the ice rink?'

'Well, thanks. It's a dream project for me.' His voice took on an intensity she had never heard before. 'I like Carl — he has a sound business mind. But Robert's another thing entirely. I heard him complaining to his mother the other day that I was sticking my nose in and cramping his style. Arnie used to give him a free rein, and Robert was saying that his dad wouldn't have liked all the changes, and outsiders running the rink.'

'Monica told me that Arnie tended to spoil Robert.'

Daniel agreed. 'Carl said as much. I

think he found his father too set in his ways latterly, and he was always resisting change. I suppose it must be galling for Robert to see someone he knew as a kid larking about on the ice now giving orders about how the place is run.' But his eyes blazed with passion as he spoke the words, and she could tell he was inspired by the challenge.

They turned off the dual carriageway and drove towards the town centre. The main street was quiet now in the late afternoon, just a few couples walking along. During shopping hours, the place was thronged with people.

'Didn't you used to have a Saturday job in one of these cafés when we were at school?' Daniel asked.

'Yes, that one over there, the Happy Teapot.' Elsa turned her head to look at the shop front, now closed for the day. 'I loved it. I even did some hours there after I started working at the building society.'

'I'm impressed. So that's where you

got the idea to run your own place?'

She grinned. Daniel was always interested in businesses. 'I realised once I started my full-time job that I was happiest in the café. The owner, Jenny, encouraged me to follow my dream. I saved hard for years. Plus being known in the building society helped me get the loan I needed.'

Daniel turned off the main road. 'When we were at school, I don't know how we managed to see each other at all, with all my skating practices.' A smile touched his mouth. 'I was a real prat then — I don't know how you put up with me.'

Elsa felt her stomach somersault, remembering the agonised teenage longing for him and the futile dreams of learning to skate. In that instant, she realised that she had never expected their romance to last. Daniel was always growing away from her. 'It was good, what we had — but it wasn't to be.'

'Elsa, I was wondering . . . '

'Oh, there's someone coming out of

my mum's house. Can you pull up here?'

'Sure, there's a space.' He edged in behind another car, where they could watch the man opening the boot of his vehicle and throwing in a sports bag.

'Is that your mum's new man?' Daniel continued as the male figure returned to the door of the house and slipped back inside.

'I'm assuming so. I'll just get out here. Thanks, Daniel. Say hello to your parents from me.'

'And the same to your mum — though I don't suppose she likes me much these days.'

Elsa bent down to look back into the car at him. 'I'm an adult now, so she can't complain about us being friends. 'Bye, see you around.'

She watched him drive off, proud of her acting skills. Hopefully he hadn't seen how churned up she felt in his presence.

When she reached the door, her mother was holding it open. After giving her daughter a hug, Rachel said, 'So who was that who dropped you off?'

Feeling as if she had been caught out, Elsa gasped. 'Daniel saw me at the bus stop, and he gave me a lift as he's going to visit his parents.' She whipped off her jacket and hung it on its usual peg in the hallway, not wanting to see her mother's expression.

'Daniel? Not Daniel Whitbridge? I thought he was married and living down south.'

Elsa tried to sound casual as she explained about his divorce and that he'd moved back to the area. 'He's involved in running the ice rink.'

'I hope he's not thinking of taking up with you again. I'll never forgive him for hurting you so badly when he left you in the lurch. You almost failed your A-levels. You could have gone to college.'

Elsa's heart sank at this tirade. It looked as if her mother would never like Daniel. 'It didn't make any difference,

Mum. I'm doing what I love — college wasn't for me. Anyway, he's involved with the new Russian coach at the ice rink, Irina.'

'I'm glad to hear it. It sounds as if he's broken another woman's heart.'

'He's changed, you know. He's grown up, just like I have.' She decided not to tell her mother about their night out, or their other meetings.

Rachel shook her head, but brightened when she opened the living room door and her eyes met those of the man who waited there. 'Elsa, this is Graham. Graham, this is my daughter.'

Tall and quite fit for a man in his sixties, Graham had short grey hair and a neat beard. His smile was generous and warm. 'Pleased to meet you Elsa. I'm not sure what's the protocol here — do we shake hands?' He looked to Rachel as if for guidance.

Despite her wariness, Elsa liked his uncertainty. She couldn't have borne it if he was overconfident. It was odd to see this strange man familiar in her mother's home, knowing where the glasses were kept, helping clear the table. Graham was quiet, not saying too much, but he brought up one or two entertaining stories about his career as a history teacher, from which he had retired the previous year.

When it was time for her bus, Rachel saw her to the door. Elsa was aware that she was waiting for a verdict. Frantically she searched for the right words as she kissed her mother's cheek. 'Graham seems nice, Mum.'

Rachel's face lit up. 'I'm so glad you like him. I hope we can all meet up again soon.'

'Yes, that would be good. 'Bye, I'll text you when I get home.' More acting! She really wanted to warn her mother not to get involved, just keep it casual. But that sounded mean and petty.

Elsa looked back at the house from the front gate. Through the living room window, she could see the silhouettes of her mother and Graham embracing. Her stomach knotted. Then as she passed his car, she felt a jolt as she remembered the holdall he'd put in the boot. Had that been an overnight bag? Were they actually . . . ?

A shudder caught her, so she banished the thoughts from her mind as she strode towards the bus stop. She wouldn't think about that now.

# 7

Two little boys raced through the doors, elbowing aside Natalie and Elsa as they rushed from the ice rink towards the outside. Natalie gave an exaggerated shudder. 'Kids! Spare me from them!'

'Just wait until you're a parent — you'll change your tune.' Zach came up behind her, his skate bag slung over his shoulder. They had just finished practising after their Sunday morning classes.

'Not me,' Natalie said under her breath as they walked into the foyer. 'Mark and I have a very nice life together with no encumbrances.'

'Zach can't wait to be an uncle.' Elsa smiled.

'Well, he'll have to find a nice girl and have some of his own,' her friend replied tartly.

Elsa laughed. Natalie always pretended to be grumpy about the kids at the rink, but she'd seen her friend smiling fondly at the tots in the Christmas skating show. They took off their warm tops and stuffed them into their bags, and Elsa returned Zach's generous grin. She believed that he was still keen on her, though he hadn't asked her out yet. She wasn't sure what she would do if he did — but maybe starting a new relationship would be the best thing to do to take her mind off Daniel. The only problem was that she liked Zach and didn't want to hurt him if she found out that he could never be more than a dear friend. The fact that he was Natalie's brother made it even more difficult.

As they threaded through the groups of people hanging round the foyer, Zach stopped suddenly, pointing to a black and orange poster on the door. 'Look, there's a Halloween ice disco on Friday. Do you fancy going, Els? That sounds like fun — fancy dress optional, but I bet you could knock up something eye-catching.'

Elsa laughed. 'It'll be full of teenagers all careering round the ice, most of them on hire skates. I don't want to come a cropper! Anyway, I've got lots of baking to do for the Saturday. I'm making decorated cupcakes and biscuits with a Halloween theme.'

'Don't be such a spoilsport! Come on, Nat, you must persuade her to come — and why don't you come too?'

Natalie had a faraway look in her eyes.

'Oh, look, she's already dreaming up a costume.'

Natalie grinned. 'Well, I sort of thought, glittery zombie bride, or something like that.'

'We'll be the only adults there!' Elsa complained.

Zach gave her a wicked look as they stepped into the open air. 'I challenge you — we'll have our own competition for the best costume.'

They waved him off on his bus while they wandered round the corner to the seafront. It was a grey day, the sea wild and forbidding. Elsa took a deep breath of the salt-laden air before saying, 'You're not serious about going to the disco, are you?'

Natalie gave a mischievous smile. 'I kind of like the idea — a bit of fun.'

'What will Mark think?'

'I'll drag him along. He'd make a great zombie bridegroom.'

Elsa giggled at the thought of quiet and gentle Mark in fancy dress. But he was so devoted to Natalie that maybe he would go along with it.

In the end, she decided to accompany her friends, and set her mind to devising a costume. Lisa looked after the café while Elsa prepared the baking for the next day. Natalie and Mark arranged to pick her up in their car. As she closed the door of her flat and walked to meet them, she heard a shriek from Natalie inside the car. 'That's a brilliant costume! A really scary witch!'

Elsa was wearing a loose black coat with a baggy black skirt to her knees, plus green and red striped tights. She had left her hair loose, letting it frizz in a mad ginger cloud round her face, which she had coloured with green make-up and red lips. She carried a crooked black witches' hat along with her skates, which she had put in a plastic bag.

'Where did you get the outfit?' Mark asked. He was wearing an old jacket and trousers, a white shirt over a sweatshirt, and sporting a giant string cobweb draped over his shoulders. Natalie was in a white dress and jumper, with another cobweb around her shoulders. She had backcombed her hair and put a large plastic spider on it. Her face was white with black-ringed eyes and red lips.

'At the charity shop on the seafront,' Elsa replied to his question. 'I bought the tights in a cheap shop in the town. Then I made the hat from cardboard and crepe paper — but I draw the line at a wart!'

Natalie guffawed. 'Pity! That would have been the crowning glory.'

Mark put the car into gear and turned out on to the main road.

'Where's Zach?'

'He's meeting us there. We'll give him a lift home later.' As soon as they turned into the car park, Natalie exclaimed, 'Look, there he is! He must have known that you were going as a witch.'

A lanky figure in a purple wizard's coat sprinkled with green stars caught their attention as they drew into the car park. He had a tall purple hat in his hand. 'Ha! I knew it!' he crowed as Elsa emerged from the car. She put her hat on her head and shook her finger at him menacingly. He struck a pose as if casting a spell.

'Right, have we all got everything? Good, let's go in. Mark will have to hire some skates.' Natalie dragged them into the queue. Thankfully there were some parents amongst the teenagers, and several other adults. The boom of music came from the ice rink, and coloured lights could be seen flashing through the glass in the doors.

Once Mark was booted up, they put all their shoes and carriers in the one bag and checked it into the cloakroom. 'This is ace,' Natalie exclaimed as they were guided on to the ice by a steward at the barrier. An array of imaginative costumes adorned the skaters, and some of the younger trained skaters were performing elaborate moves as they followed the crowd anti-clockwise round the ice. One or two would peel off from time to time to execute a spin or jump in the central section.

Elsa had to admit that she was glad she had come. It had been fun dressing up, something she hadn't done for years, and they all laughed and fooled about in their characters. Natalie held on to Mark, who was making a decent attempt to skate round. She shouted over the music that she had been making him practise the right moves in their kitchen. Zach skated with Elsa, making wizardly actions towards her, while she pulled witchy faces and cast spells at him.

After a while it became more crowded, and there had been a few spectacular trips and falls nearby, so Zach gesticulated to them that they should go off next time they passed the entrance. Laughing, they stumbled on to the rubber matting.

'There are still people arriving — how many are they going to allow in?' Elsa wondered as they made their way through to the cafeteria.

'I'm sure that there must be a limit,' Mark said, walking awkwardly in his hire skates. 'How do you make it look so easy? My legs will be screaming tomorrow.'

'Don't worry, at least you're not covered in bruises like I was after my first few times on the ice.' Zach took off his hat and scratched his head, making his hair stand up on end.

'I'm a very good teacher,' Natalie added, checking that her spider was still in her bouffant hair. 'Now what are we having to drink?'

'I could do with a beer,' Zach stated.

'No alcohol, of course — it doesn't go with the ice.'

'More's the pity,' Mark commented. 'Is the bar open later? Can you use it, as members of the club?'

'Maybe — we can see.'

After getting some cool drinks at the café, they returned to the disco and attempted to dance in their costumes, before it came to ten o'clock and the event closed down. They were the last in the queue at the cloakroom, as there had been a mix-up with Mark's shoes at the skate hire, and it had taken the attendant some time to find them.

'Shall we see if the bar's open?' Zach laced up his trainers.

Wiping the dampness off her blades, Elsa reached into her bag for her 'soakers', fleecy covers that drew off the moisture from the blades. 'We could try. What do you two think?'

'Well, if it's not open, we can just go to a pub somewhere. Natalie?' Mark looked to his wife, who gave a murmur of agreement.

The corridor had grown quiet now. They headed off past the skate hire booth, now locked up. Coming through the doors, Elsa could see two tall figures ahead of them at the doors to the stairs that would go up to the bar. Zach headed towards them cheerfully.

'They look a bit grim,' Natalie said under her breath as the two men turned toward them. They were wearing Frankenstein's monster masks that covered the whole of their heads.

'Zach . . . ' Elsa felt suddenly nervous, trying to draw him back. But she was too late.

'Hi, guys, is the bar open?' Zach asked in his typically open manner.

'No.' They stood as if guarding the stairs.

'Oh, we thought it might be. Are you

sure?' Zach stepped forward before anyone could stop him, at which one of the men reached out and gave him a push in the chest.

'Back off. We said it was closed.' The voice was harsh.

'Come on, now.' Zach threw up his hands.

'Zach, come away.' Elsa, frightened, ran forward to take his arm.

'I said back off,' the gruff voice said, and he lunged at Zach.

He stumbled backwards, gripping his arm. The two men disappeared through the door, but stood looking through at them through the glass.

Mark took the women's arms and hustled them back along the corridor. 'I don't like that at all. I'm going to report it in the box office.'

'Wait . . . wait, there's something wrong with Zach.' Natalie wrenched from his grip and ran back to her brother, who was bending over, holding his arm.

A red streak appeared on Natalie's

white dress. 'Nat . . . I . . . I think I'm bleeding,' Zach croaked, and promptly passed out.

# 8

'Zach!' Natalie screamed, trying to hold him upright.

Mark released Elsa's arm and ran to help Natalie. They laid Zach on the rubber matting while Elsa pulled back his sleeve. There was a gash about ten centimetres long in his forearm. She pulled off her coat, and then her T-shirt, which she scrunched up into a ball and pressed against the wound.

There was the sound of the door opening further towards the box office. 'We're closing now, you have to . . . Oh my goodness, what's happened?' Jean paused, horrified, at the scene before her. Elsa's T-shirt was already turning red, and the dramatic stain down Natalie's dress looked horrific.

'My brother-in-law was set upon by two men in masks down the corridor. They've stabbed him, and as you can

121

see, he's losing quite a lot of blood.' Mark was holding Natalie's shoulders as she sobbed.

'I'll call an ambulance — and the police.' As she turned on her heel, a man appeared from the same direction. 'Oh, Daniel, there's been an attack down the corridor. Someone's been knifed!'

Elsa looked up with relief to see Daniel hurrying towards them. He checked suddenly, his face draining of colour as he registered that it was Elsa with her friends. 'Elsa, are you hurt?'

'It's my brother! Help him, please!' Natalie's voice was panicky.

Daniel's mouth set in a firm line. 'Is he badly hurt?' He seemed to regain his composure and hurried towards them.

'No, I don't think so, but he's in shock and is losing a fair amount of blood,' Elsa said.

'Here, let me see.' Daniel knelt down and eased back the T-shirt cloth. 'Yes, it's still bleeding. Keep pressing on the wound, and try to keep him warm.

What happened?'

With a shaking voice, Elsa outlined the series of events.

As soon as she finished, Daniel jumped to his feet. 'I'm going to see if the attacker's still there.'

'Daniel, be careful — there were two of them, and they weren't afraid to come at us, with both Mark and Zach.'

'I'll go with you,' Mark offered.

'No, don't risk it!' Natalie grabbed his arm.

'To be honest, I don't think they'll be there.' Mark stroked his wife's arm. 'They're not going to hang around when they know that we'll raise the alarm. We won't go near them, Natalie, but I think this guy should have someone at his back.'

Daniel nodded. 'Don't worry, we won't approach them. I need to see if I recognise them.'

The two men disappeared back along the corridor, while Natalie and Elsa remained with Zach in the semi-dark and the cold. At that moment, Zach gave a groan.

'Zach, can you hear me? Are you all right?'

The prostrate figure swore under his breath. 'What the hell happened? My arm's on fire!'

'Don't try to move. Help's on its way.' Elsa stopped him moving his arm, holding the T-shirt firm.

A minute later, the doors opened and Daniel and Mark returned, grim-faced. 'We went right up the stairs but there was no sign of them. The bar's locked. We'd better wait now until the police arrive, and let them search the whole building. I think we should move you all to the foyer, especially as Jean's on her own there. All the other staff have gone home now. Can you walk?' He bent to Zach.

'I . . . think so. I'm just a bit shaky, you know. I'm not really good with blood.' He studiously turned his head away from the blood-soaked covering on his arm.

124

Daniel and Mark helped him along the corridor, until they reached the tiny room used by the box office staff. Jean came in with a blanket as they laid Zach on an old settee in the corner. It was warm in there, which was just as well as he had begun to shiver. 'A paramedic is coming, and the police are on their way as well — but it could be a while, being Friday night. And here was I thinking we'd got off lightly tonight, with no serious tumbles on the ice.' Her lips twitched sympathetically. She bound Zach's arm firmly with bandages over Elsa's T-shirt and advised him to rest his hand against his shoulder. Then she went back to the front of the building to wait for the emergency services.

'She seems very calm about it.' Natalie huddled into Mark's embrace.

'The box office staff are used to dealing with blood and gore — after all, there are often broken wrists and other cuts and bruises to deal with. Jean's been with the rink for years, and she's a tower of strength.'

It wasn't long until the paramedics arrived, and they took Zach to the hospital for stitching. Natalie insisted on accompanying him, while Mark and Elsa waited in the office with Daniel. Despite the coffee Daniel had brought from a vending machine, exhaustion was beginning to overwhelm her. When the telephone on the desk rang, they all jumped.

'Hello?' Daniel grabbed the receiver. 'Well, you'll just have to tell them that they'll have to wait until the police arrive and search the building. Though I'm sure that the culprits are long gone. Still, I don't want any more attacks.' He paused, listening to the voice on the other end. 'Okay, you can send Andrew in. Tell him to come to the downstairs office.' He replaced the receiver. 'There are some ice hockey players turning up for their practice, which starts at eleven o'clock. As there's a match on Sunday evening, they're anxious not to miss their ice time.'

The door swung open, and Andrew, Daniel's younger brother, entered. His eyes widened when he saw Elsa. 'Hi, Daniel, Elsa — what's going on?'

Daniel just had time to outline what had happened, when the door opened again to reveal two muscular police-men. Daniel explained again about the attack on Zach, and took the officers to show them where it had occurred.

Andrew settled down on one of the spare seats. 'How are you, Elsa? Daniel mentioned that he'd met you here as you'd taken up skating.'

'Yes, but it's turned out to be rather more exciting than I would have liked.' She pulled her black coat round herself, beginning to feel rather foolish in her Halloween outfit. Why on earth had she chosen to have a green face?

'So you were at the Halloween disco?'

Mark had taken off his cobweb, so was looking more normal. He nodded. 'Yes, though I wish now we'd never come. I hope the police will talk to us soon, so that I can go and join Natalie at the hospital.'

'How does your family feel about you doing late night sessions at the ice rink?' Elsa asked Andrew.

He grinned. 'The kids always want to come with me when I'm training, but when it's late they're usually asleep in bed, so I can sneak out without them knowing. They both went trick-or-treating earlier, so they were worn out and went straight to sleep.'

'How's Poppy getting on? She was marvellous at the annual competition.'

'Yes, she adores skating, and I think she's going to stick at it. My boy, Ryan, is just as mad about ice hockey. He's nine next month, and can chase a puck as well as a twelve-year-old.' His voice oozed pride.

The door opened again, revealing Daniel with a police officer. 'The officer will take your statements now, then you can go. I'm sorry you had to wait.'

'I take it you didn't find anything?' Mark asked.

Daniel looked grave. 'No, though I wasn't too surprised. There was plenty of time for them to make their escape. The fire door at the back looked as if it wasn't properly sealed. That's something else we need to address.'

'The list keeps growing.' Andrew stood up. 'I think we could start the training session now?'

'Yes, go ahead,' the officer said, taking his place.

It was another thirty minutes before Elsa and Mark were able to leave. Daniel hurried to speak with them as they were heading for the door.

'Elsa! Are you all right?'

She looked at him wearily. 'It's been a long night. We've described the incident and the appearance of the men in as much detail as we could — which wasn't really a help, as their masks were a good disguise. Mark's going to take me home before going on to the hospital.'

Daniel touched her arm gently. 'I'm so sorry this happened. We thought we had good security, but obviously we need to do better.' He gave a brief smile. 'Go home, have something warm to drink, and cuddle your cat. Then try to get some sleep.'

She nodded, touched that he should remember about Missy. Yes, that would be the best thing to do.

Somehow Elsa managed to get some sleep that night, but wakened early. Although she was desperate to know how Zach was, she resisted telephoning Natalie early, instead sending her a text. She had plenty to do before opening the café as she had advertised pumpkin soup for Saturday lunch, which needed preparing.

The soup was simmering on the cooker when her mobile rang.

'Natalie, how's Zach?'

'They gave him some stitches and painkillers, but said that he could go home, so we brought him back here. I've told him he's to stay with us tonight as well, and then see how he feels tomorrow. He'll have a bit of a job looking after himself with his arm in a sling.'

Elsa worried about Zach for the rest of the day, feeling as if she was on automatic pilot. She was thankful that Lisa and Katy were full of energy and had bright faces for the customers.

Although she was tempted to go round to see her friends that evening, she thought that Zach would need to rest, so decided just to curl up on the settee to watch *Strictly Come Dancing* with Missy snuggled in beside her. Unfortunately, the fabulous Halloween costumes that the dancers and celebrities were wearing just reminded her of last night. She was glad when the programme finished, and she managed to find a romantic comedy film on another channel.

At half past nine, her phone rang. 'Hello, Elsa, it's Daniel. How are you, after last night? How's your friend?'

Surprised yet gratified, Elsa began to unwind for the first time that day as she told him what she knew about Zach.

Then they chatted a bit about the ice rink before Daniel said, 'Well, I'm glad you're not too freaked out. It must have been frightening. I'm going to divert some of our funds and energies into promoting better security as from this week. I'll see you around the rink sometime. Bye.'

A pang of regret caught Elsa at his casual manner towards her. Shaking herself, she told herself that it was natural, as he was with Irina, wasn't he? Then a thought struck her — was he under the impression that Zach was her boyfriend? For that matter, *was* he? Unable to give herself a clear answer, she sighed and turned to the sleeping cat, stroking her warm fur. Then she reached for the TV remote control and set the movie to play again. At least she could enjoy a fictitious happy ending, even if her own love life was such a mess.

# 9

Monica rang on the Sunday evening, concerned because Daniel had mentioned the incident at the ice rink. After they had talked a little, the older woman told Elsa that she shouldn't think of coming into the shop the next day.

'Susan did absolutely fine on her first day last week, and she worked this morning as well. I'm so glad we chose her to be my assistant. She's a quick study, and so good with the computer.'

A week before, Elsa would have felt disappointed as she had enjoyed her time helping out. But knowing that she didn't have to go to the ice rink lifted a load from her shoulders. 'Thanks, Monica. It was frightening on Friday, and it would be nice to do something completely different. I think I might go for a walk on the beach if the weather's dry.'

The Wednesday after the incident, Elsa was in the café on her own, it being Lisa's day off, and Katy was busy. Just after four o'clock, when she was ringing up a payment from a young mother with a pushchair, she heard the 'ting' of the door as it admitted Tara, Monica's granddaughter. She was wearing warm leggings and a sweatshirt, and paused to boost her skating trolley bag over the lip of the door.

Tara sometimes helped out in the ice rink shop on a Sunday, and Elsa often had a chat with her. Today she appeared a little hesitant, her gaze darting round the café, taking in the elderly couple at the table near the counter, and a younger woman reading a novel while drinking a coffee.

'Hello, Tara. What can I do for you?'

The girl's head snapped round. 'I've got an extra lesson with Irina at five o'clock, but I'd like something to keep me going until I get home later. Could I have a hot chocolate and . . . ' She scrutinised the cakes behind the glass counter. 'An almond and apricot slice, please?'

Elsa dished up her request and brought it over to the table by the window where the young girl had taken a seat. They made some conversation about the smell of new paint that seemed to pervade everywhere at the ice rink these days. She had learned not to mention Bethany to Tara, as a fierce rivalry had sprung up between the two girls. But before they could talk further, the bell on the café door sounded again.

A tall young man came through the door, his blond hair tousled, carrying a skating bag. Around the same age as Tara and Bethany, he was wearing a dark hoodie and trousers. His face lit up when he looked in their direction. 'Hi, Tara. I didn't know that you came here. I heard about this café and how good the cakes are.'

Tara dropped her fork and bent to

pick it up, her face glowing pink. As she surfaced, she managed to stammer, 'Hello, Jacob. Yes, it's really nice here. I'm just having something to eat before my lesson.'

Elsa took the fork. 'I'll get you a clean one'.

'Jacob, this is Elsa, who runs the café — and bakes the cakes.'

So this was Jacob Hurwell, the young skater who had followed Irina to Heronsburn so that he could keep training with her. He followed Elsa over to the counter and chose a flapjack.

'Could you put it in a bag for me, please? My lesson starts at 4.30. And would it be OK to have a coffee to go as well?'

'No problem,' Elsa stated, reaching for a paper cup and lid. She could see Tara's face falling when she heard that Jacob wouldn't be staying.

After he had gone, Elsa took a clean fork over to Tara and ventured, 'He looks nice.'

'Yes, he is.' Tara cut a slice of her cake

with a trembling hand. 'Though I'm lucky that Bethany wasn't here, otherwise she wouldn't have let me have a look-in.'

'Is he her boyfriend?'

'No, but she'd like to think so. He's a really brilliant skater, and he's complimented me on my skating, too. I like him.'

'As in *like* rather than just 'like'?'

Tara grinned, lowering her eyelashes. 'You might say that.' She looked up, her cheeks pink. 'Oh, Elsa, he's absolutely gorgeous, and so kind. I hope Bethany doesn't get her claws into him. She's bad enough as it is, but if she had him, too, she would be unbearable.'

'I'll keep my fingers crossed for you.' Elsa liked the girl, and felt that Tara deserved something good, after losing her grandfather in such tragic circumstances.

The following Saturday there was a volunteer beach clean-up at Heronsburn. The council had instigated it the previous year, and it had proved to be popular, helping the beach get blue flag status. Clean beach status had been difficult to achieve because of the industrial past of the coast, which had been a coal-mining area, but at long last they had succeeded.

The council had laid on a refreshment tent for the volunteers, but the café also was doing a roaring trade that day. Natalie and Mark would be taking part, so Elsa slipped out during her lunch break, leaving the café in the capable hands of Lisa and Katy.

It was a breezy day, but dry. Leaning on the painted railings, Elsa took a deep breath of salt-laden air. The tide was far out, streaked with white horses. The beach was strewn with the occasional piece of dried seaweed, and was dotted with pebbles near the promenade. Other people strolled along, families and people walking their dogs. The volunteers had been working since nine thirty, as the tide was on its way out then. Elsa shielded her eyes from the sun as she gazed to the south, and spied a crowd of people of various ages wearing yellow tabards and carrying huge sacks and picking sticks. They were offloading their sacks into some large wheelie bins. They must be finished already.

She decided to walk in that direction, and spied a tall man with his arm in a sling walking towards her. Delighted, she recognised that it was Zach, and waved at him.

'Hi, Elsa! They're finished now, and they're going up to the refreshment tent.'

'How's the arm?' she asked as she fell into step beside him.

He admitted that he was using it a lot more now. 'I'm just glad that this isn't going to affect my trip to Australia in January. I've been planning it for a year, and I'd be gutted if I had to cancel.'

'How long are you going for?'

'Lucky sod, he's going for a whole month!' Natalie had reached them, and was pulling off her tabard. 'Can't wait to get rid of this — not the best fashion statement of the year.'

'I had to save up last year's leave as well as this year's. I've been planning this holiday for two years.'

Mark came up behind Natalie and took the yellow garment from her. 'I'll just go and hand these back. Are you going to the tent?'

'Yes, we'll see you there. I need warming up. I was hot while I was working, but I'm feeling chilly now.' Natalie was wearing a thick fleece and woolly hat. She blew on her hands, then reached into her pocket for a pair of gloves.

All of them except Elsa grabbed a paper cup of warm tea or coffee. Natalie cradled it gratefully. 'Ooh, that's better. Has it been busy in the café today, Elsa?'

'More customers than usual, certainly. I can't stay long, as we have to clear tables as quickly as possible.'

'Well, before you dash off, I want to ask you something. As Zach can't skate for the next few weeks, how about us going to an ice hockey match? Mark suggested it, as he's gone right off skating himself. What do you think?'

'Ice hockey? That might be fun. I've watched it on television at the Winter Olympics, and it looked exciting. Are the Heronsburn Hawks any good?'

'Yeah — they're near the top of their league; I looked it up.' Zach drained his coffee. 'The match is on Sunday, at 7.30.'

'Go on, then. I'm game.'

The following week they met outside the ice rink, wrapped up in hats, scarves and woolly gloves. Zach's arm was out of its sling. Natalie and Mark were wearing their skiing clothes. 'Including thermals,' she added.

They joined the queue, and Elsa was astonished when they entered the rink to find it full of spectators, with high-energy music blaring through the sound system. They made their way to their seats, high up the tiered rows.

Soon the match started, and they joined in cheering for their local side, the Heronsburn Hawks. It was exciting, the players skating round at speed, nimbly circling opponents, or clashing with their sticks or bodies. Both sides had scored three goals by half-time.

Natalie's face was glowing. 'Hey, this is really exciting! Why didn't we think of doing this before?'

'You're not going to take up ice hockey, now, are you?' Elsa laughed over the noise of the music.

'Women do play, you know.'

'So is it a pair of ice hockey skates for Christmas, then?' Mark grinned, putting his arm round his wife's waist and hugging her to him.

'You would be good at that, you know. You did very well on your hire skates.'

'Oh, no, I'm not skating any more. I'm leaving that to you two.'

They decided to queue for some drinks, as their throats were parched after shouting for the team. Elsa excused herself to slip away to the Ladies' room while they were waiting.

When she emerged, she almost bumped into Daniel, who was walking past with an older man. She remembered he was Byron Newminster, one of the consortium.

'Hello, Elsa. I didn't know that you were an ice hockey fan,' Daniel said. Newminster nodded briefly at her and carried on walking, leaving them to talk.

'It's my first time, and I'm enjoying it. I've come with Natalie, Mark and Zach.'

'How's your boyfriend's arm?'

Horrified at his assumption, she blurted, 'Zach's not my boyfriend! He's Natalie's brother, and a friend.'

'Oh, I'm sorry — it was just that you always seemed so close whenever I saw you together.'

She sighed. How could she explain that Zach had fancied her for ages, and she really couldn't make up her mind about him, because she had admitted to herself that a part of her still wanted Daniel. 'It doesn't matter. Anyway,

Zach's arm is much better, but he won't be skating for a while. The next half is about to start, and your colleague is waiting for you.'

Reluctantly, she pulled away and ran along the corridor to her block of seating. Zach waved at her as she reached them. 'There you are! We thought you'd got lost. Here's your drink.'

Thanking him, she slipped into the seat beside him and began to sip her drink. But her thoughts were no longer on the game. Even though the team won by six to four, she was distracted by her meeting with Daniel. He knew now that she wasn't going out with Zach, but as far as she knew he was still involved with Irina. She really must try and quell these feelings that had resurfaced.

Sunday classes were now taken up with rehearsing for the Christmas show, which the coaches said would be bigger and better this year. At their next Sunday morning class, it was a surprise to find Irina in place of their usual coach, Laura.

'Laura's not well,' Fiona said as they began their warm-up, skating backwards and forwards across their section of the ice rink. Irina snapped one instruction after another without a break, urging them to go faster, make bigger movements, and gave them some complicated arm gestures to do while they were skating. After what seemed like a gruelling ten minutes, they gathered round her, out of breath.

'Now, I understand that Laura has been rehearsing a routine with you. What's your music?'

'It's *Cabaret*,' Fiona said.

'Ah, I see. Well, get into place; I want to see how you are getting on.'

They went through the routine as best they could, but Elsa was aware of Irina's frowning face the whole time she was skating, which made her feel tense. Three of their number were missing that morning, all of whom were on one side as they divided, and this meant that their pairs were often singles. Elsa fluffed her jump, landing awkwardly. She muttered crossly under her breath. Irina was sure to have noticed.

'What are those gaps?' The coach's heavily accented voice lashed at them as they finished. 'It looks very ragged. You must make it much better for the show.'

Natalie explained about the absent participants.

'You must be flexible,' Irina scolded. 'What if these people are missing on the day of the show? Now, get back into lines to start. You must all take a partner, even if it is not your usual one. When you divide, do not go to your usual side if there is someone missing in front of you — divide evenly. Now, once more, go!'

They went through the routine several more times. Fiona stayed back for a moment to do some moves that she needed to perform for her next assessment, due that morning.

'Phew! I don't think I've ever worked so hard.' Natalie stepped back on to the side of the rink, Elsa at her heels.

'She was right, though. We have to be prepared in case someone doesn't come to the performance.'

'But she could be nicer about it. What a slave driver!'

Watching the coach as she began the next class of adults, Elsa wondered what Irina was like in her private life. Daniel must like that type of driven person — after all, he had been attracted to Hannah, another successful and strong woman. In comparison, Elsa regarded herself as a stay-at-home who was quite happy with her café.

She was still trying to cheer herself up that evening, watching Sunday night television with Missy beside her, and wondering if she should have taken up Zach's offer to go out for a drink. The telephone rang, so she reached for it and answered.

'Is that the Rainbow Café? Am I speaking to Elsa Turnfield?' It was a man's voice, unfamiliar, with the hint of a local accent.

'Yes it is.' Elsa always switched the café phone through to her flat when the premises closed.

'My name is Nathan Troutbeck. I'm a journalist with the *Northern County News*. I'm sorry to disturb you on a Sunday evening, but I hoped I would catch you in. I'm doing some interviews with local businesses that have set up within the past few years and are doing well. It's to encourage other people to start new businesses, and also to promote sponsorship. Success stories are always good for the local economy, and it could bring you new customers as well.'

'That sounds interesting.'

'I was wondering if I could come and interview you — preferably when the café is open, so that I can write about it.'

'Yes, that's possible. Wednesday morning is usually quiet. We open at ten thirty in winter.'

'I'll be along then. See you on Wednesday.'

An article in the local paper! Plus, she was seen to be a success story! Suddenly her spirits soared. She wasn't such a failure after all.

# 10

Wednesday was surprisingly busy for a November weekday, which meant that Elsa and Lisa were almost run off their feet. Elsa quickly prepared some salads for lunchtime, as she didn't know how long the journalist's interview would take.

A dark-haired man with a beard came up to the counter with his bill. 'I really enjoyed that fruitcake. Did you make it yourself?'

She took the proffered note and rang up the sale on the till. 'Yes, I make all of the cakes, and my assistant helps with the lunchtime sandwiches and salads.'

When she handed him his change, he was holding out a card. 'Nathan Troutbeck, *Northern County News*. I decided to start incognito as I wanted to see you at work without you feeling self-conscious. I must say, I'm impressed.'

Flustered, Elsa wiped her hands down her red work apron. 'Oh, well, thank you. Would you like to come up to the flat? Lisa can take over now, if she's finished making sandwiches.'

They climbed the stairs to the flat. Missy took one look at the visitor and shot out of the door. He grinned. 'I probably smell of dog — I was walking my Labrador this morning.'

'Do you live locally?'

'I live on the other side of the city, but I often cover the stories in Heronsburn. It's part of my patch.'

Elsa gave a small smile to herself. She always thought of a 'patch' now as a skating session. She showed him to an armchair, glad that she had tidied and vacuumed that morning to remove most of the cat hair. Missy always seemed to moult, regardless of the season. 'I won't offer you a coffee, seeing as you've just had one.'

He took out a small recording device

and placed it on the coffee table. 'I hope you don't mind — I take some notes, but it's helpful to be able to play an interview back, just to make sure I get facts right.'

Impressed, Elsa nodded. 'So, what do you want to know?'

He encouraged her to talk about her background, and how she had set up the business. He knew exactly the right questions to ask, and even had her thinking on her feet a few times with queries that she had not anticipated.

After about forty five minutes, he declared himself satisfied with the information he had gleaned. 'Just one thing,' he said as he was packing away the recorder. 'What's your involvement with Daniel Whitbridge, the new manager of Heronsburn Ice Rink?'

For a moment the breath felt as if it was knocked out of her. Then she managed to stammer, '*Daniel?* What's he to do with anything? He's an old friend, I knew him at school.' Anger flared in her.

Nathan looked at her, his face suddenly less friendly. 'I saw you deep in conversation at the ice hockey match last week. You looked as if you were in a serious discussion. Plus, you work at the ice rink sometimes. You must know what's going on behind the scenes?'

'I don't know what you mean!' Furious, she stood up, and he mirrored her action.

'And I gather you were involved in an incident at the ice rink a few weeks ago. Don't you think that there's something sinister going on, and it seems to have started when Daniel Whitbridge returned to the area?'

'Daniel's not crooked, if that's what you're implying. He just wants to make a go of the ice rink. He's an honest businessman!' She stalked to the door. 'The interview is over! If you write anything about me and the ice rink, I'll sue you!' She wasn't sure if she could, but in her anger she just wanted to get rid of this man.

He gave a smile — a rather menacing

one, she thought. 'No, I'll run the interview as it stands. I'm genuinely doing articles on local businesses. But if you discover anything about the ice rink, I hope you'll contact me. I'll leave you my card.' He held it out, and when she failed to take it, laid it on the coffee table before walking to the door. 'Thank you for your time, Miss Turnfield.'

Once he had left the room, Elsa closed the door firmly, resting her head against it. All the euphoria she had previously felt was now gone, in its place a sickening dread. What had this man seen, and was there more going on at the ice rink than she had previously imagined? Turning on her heel, she went to find her mobile phone, and dialled.

'Daniel? It's Elsa. I need to see you. There's a journalist been asking me questions about you and the ice rink. I thought he wanted to interview me about my business, but it seems that he had an ulterior motive.'

'What sort of questions? Was he threatening?'

'No, he didn't threaten me. He actually says that he's going to run the article about the café. But I didn't like the questions he asked me at the end. He implied that something nasty was afoot at the ice rink, though he didn't say what.'

There was a pause at the other end of the line. 'I'm tied up for most of the day, but I'm free later. Would you like to have a pub meal with me? I'm expected back at the rink for a meeting with the consortium at 8.30, but if we get a table at 6.30 we should be finished in plenty of time.'

They agreed that he would pick her up at a quarter past six. That day her last customers left the café at ten past five, so she turned the sign to 'Closed' and set to with her cleaning materials. While she wiped the tables and counter, then washed over the floor with a squeezy mop, her mind was going over what she should wear. It shouldn't really matter, she told herself, but she couldn't help wanting to look her best with Daniel. She wanted to show him that she was a mature adult with style, not the gawky redhead he had known all those years ago.

By only giving the kitchen a cursory wipe (she would do it properly in the morning, she promised herself), she had fifteen minutes to race upstairs, have a five-minute wash in the bathroom, and throw on a pair of cinnamon-coloured trousers with a cream cardigan. Combing her hair, she deftly put it into a loose plait, then reapplied her make-up, with just a touch of mascara and a pale peach lip gloss. Lastly, she changed her earrings to a pair of small pearl studs that her brother had given her for her birthday that year. At that moment she heard the sound of a car drawing into the side street, so she grabbed her bag and her brown leather jacket.

'Phew, I didn't have much time to get ready.' She ran round the car and jumped into the passenger seat.

Daniel grinned. 'Well, I must say you've done a great job.'

His comment gave her a warm feeling. 'It makes a pleasant change to get out of the black that I wear in the café. Although we do wear coloured aprons to keep the rainbow theme.'

With a smile, he put the car into gear and set off. Elsa sat back and enjoyed the sensation of being near him. That little flutter within her started again. He drove for about ten minutes inland, before stopping at a pub restaurant from a popular chain. A young waitress showed them to a table near the window, which wasn't near any occupied ones, so they would be able to talk without being overheard. Once they had chosen their drinks and placed their order, Daniel put his elbows on the table and leaned forward slightly.

'So this journalist — what was his name?'

'He gave me a card.' Elsa fished in

her shoulder bag, and handed the card to him.

'Nathan Troutbeck. It doesn't ring a bell, though I'm not familiar with the local press. I haven't bought this paper recently.' He returned the card to her.

'I buy it occasionally.' Elsa tucked it back in her handbag. 'He seemed genuine enough, and I thought he was quite skilled in interviewing. Though I suppose anyone could have a card printed with their name on.'

'We'll need to see if the article does appear in the newspaper. What sort of age was he?'

'Similar to us, I thought. So I expect he's still climbing up the ladder. How do you think he's cottoned on to something going on at the ice rink?'

Daniel laced his fingers and laid his chin on them, not looking directly at her. After a moment, he said, 'I suppose he's just putting two and two together. I must say, I'm not surprised. First, Arnie's unexpected death, then the incident with your friend a few weeks back. Plus, there's always coming and going at odd times of the day and night, with all the private sessions such as patches and team training for the Heronsburn Hawks. People are always surprised that the ice rink stays open most of the twenty four hours.'

'Monica was saying that she kept seeing strange men around, but she couldn't be sure if they were just involved in the renovations.'

'I know; we're rather open just now.'

At that moment, the waitress brought their meals, so they sat back while she laid the steaming plates on the table.

'This looks good,' Daniel said as he unwrapped his cutlery from the paper napkin and applied it to his steak.

Elsa nodded, cutting a piece of her chicken in creamy sauce. 'I'm suddenly ravenous. It's been a busy day.' They were silent for a few moments while they began to eat.

'I don't know whether it's significant or not, but once or twice in the past few months, I've heard a large lorry turning in my side street in the middle of the night. My bedroom faces that direction. I looked out a couple of times, and it was going towards the ice rink.' She didn't mention that the last time she had watched from her window, the lorry driver had looked up at her with a surly glare, making her start back, alarmed.

Daniel frowned, spearing some winter greens with his fork. 'Well, we don't know for sure that it has anything to do with the rink. I'm reluctant to believe that there's really any connection between the incidents. I know that Arnie was in financial trouble, and it was taking a lot of persuasion to let me in. It's perfectly plausible that he could have just been at a low ebb because he felt he had failed, and couldn't go on. Those two intruders at the ice rink could have been looking for something to pinch, though what anyone would think they could find there, I don't know. And Monica's strange men could be workmen, and the lorries you heard could have been making deliveries, either to the ice rink or somewhere else.'

'I suppose so.' Though she did remember seeing those shifty men when she was on her own in the corridor. Maybe they were having a sly drink at work.

'Thanks for telling me, anyway. I'll keep my eyes open for this reporter. What did he look like?'

Elsa described him as well as she could. Daniel nodded, and continued with his meal. He began to ask her about her skating, so she told him about the Christmas show.

'Irina was coaching us last week — she's very thorough, isn't she?'

He laughed. 'That's her all over. She's a perfectionist, and at times can seem strict, but she gets results, as can be seen from her students. Even Tara had a higher place in the British championships this year.'

Taking a deep breath, Elsa decided

that she needed to know more about Daniel and Irina. 'Did you know her in London?'

'Yes, I used to go to the ice rink where she was a coach. I noticed immediately how good she was. I was surprised that she wasn't still competing herself, but I learned that she'd come to England to be with an ice hockey player she'd become involved with in Russia. He took a contract with a club in this country, and when she discovered she was pregnant, she came with him.'

'I didn't realise she had a child.' Irina didn't seem to be the motherly type.

'Yes, Dmitri is seven. Unfortunately her relationship with his father didn't work out, but she decided to stay, as she was working here and felt that he was getting good care.'

'Care?'

'Yes, Dmitri has cerebral palsy. He can't walk very well, and as he's getting older he spends more time in a wheelchair. He's had one or two operations. But he's a lovely, happy boy. Irina's absolutely devoted to him. He's started at the local school this term, and is doing well.'

So *that* was why Irina was at the school fete in the summer.

'When I was thinking about someone for head coach, I knew about her record of success, but it was also in my mind that the extra money would help with the care he needs.'

'Poor Irina — how tragic that her little boy is so handicapped.' Elsa was beginning to see the coach in a different light.

'She doesn't feel sorry for herself, though she regrets that her boy has a hard time. I admire her very much. I suppose it was inevitable that we would become involved after my marriage broke down.'

Looking into his eyes, Elsa understood that his feelings for Irina were genuine, and felt her heart sink. He had put her fears into words. There was no room for Elsa in his life, now. She was just the ex-girlfriend from the past, a childhood romance that had gone wrong.

They settled the bill and went back to the car. 'I'm very impressed with your café, Elsa. I keep meaning to sample your wares, but it's been manic for the past few months. I hope you get your article, to bring in even more business.'

She smiled, though inside she was numb, knowing that they must be nothing more than friends. 'Please do call in. You can try my carrot cake, it's a speciality. Tuesday and Saturday for that.'

They drew up outside the café. Elsa put her hand on the car door to make a quick getaway, as she could feel a lump rising in her throat. But before she could grasp the handle, she felt Daniel's hand on her arm.

'Elsa . . . '

She whipped her head round to look into his face, and for a moment was mesmerised by the intensity in his eyes.

His hand felt like a hot coal on her arm through her sleeve. Oh, how she wished she could give in to the emotions that were surging inside her. This wasn't like a teenage crush — they had grown up, experienced loss, and if she gave rein to her feelings they could be so much deeper. If only he wasn't involved with someone else.

'Could we do this again? I'd really like to . . . '

A stab of anger caught her. Did he think she was going to be some kind of bit on the side, his old flame as a spare part? 'Sorry Daniel, I've got to go. It's been a nice evening, but Missy is waiting for me. Goodnight.'

Elsa flung open the door and leaped out of the car without registering his reaction to her words. The bite of the wind laced with icy rain made her draw her breath sharply as it hit the exposed skin of her face. With gritted teeth she hurried towards her door. Within seconds she had slotted her key into the lock and slipped inside, and was listening to the sound of his car driving away. Only then did she drop her face into her hands and let the tears overflow from her eyes, the pain of loss ripping into her chest. The part of her life that contained Daniel was gone forever.

# 11

Elsa couldn't work up the enthusiasm to go to the ice rink for her skating lesson the following Sunday. Natalie called in on her way home, to find her serving coffees to the usual bunch of Sunday morning strollers and dog walkers.

Stalking up to the counter, Natalie said, 'I'll have a large latte, if you don't mind, and one of those pink cupcakes — but only if you explain why you didn't come this morning. I thought you must be ill.'

Sighing, Elsa put the cake on a plate and made the coffee, which she brought to the table where Natalie was sitting, with her skating bag on the floor beside her.

'Well, come on, what's up? You look as if you've lost a diamond and found a pebble.' Natalie took a sip of the coffee, then a large bite of the cupcake. 'Too much baking?'

Elsa looked at her hands, unsure what to say. 'No, it's not that — not the business, anyway.'

Her friend cocked her head. 'Well, if it's not work, it must be a man — though why that should affect your skating, I don't know. It can't be Zach, because he's not at the ice rink. For that matter, what about you and Zach? Has he cracked through your shell yet?'

'No, not Zach. I'm very fond of him, but I just don't fancy him — yet. Maybe in time.'

Natalie finished the cupcake and wiped her fingers on the paper napkin. 'Well, if it's not my brother, it must be someone else who's giving you such a long face — someone at the ice rink? Though how you managed it without me noticing, I don't know.'

With a sigh, Elsa twisted her hands in her lap. 'I suppose I'd better explain.' She turned her head to check that Lisa and Katy were managing all right before launching into the story of her teenage romance with Daniel. Then she told how he'd shown some interest in her after he returned, but she had suspected that he was involved with Irina. 'And he confirmed it to me on Tuesday. I know it's stupid, but I just can't face going to the rink in case I see him there, and I don't want to bump into Irina either.'

'Well, he's not worth worrying about, as he obviously goes for these tough career women.'

'So what am I?' Elsa bridled.

Natalie drained her coffee. 'You're a career woman — but you're not tough. You've got a soft centre.'

'Well, it seems that Irina has a soft centre too.' Elsa explained about her little boy.

Natalie's eyes widened. 'Well, that explains a lot. I suppose she has to be focused because she's a single mother with a disabled child. She has guts.'

'Daniel says he's a great kid — I know he loves children, and wants some of his own. He's very close to his niece and nephew.'

Natalie leaned over and gave her a hug. 'Well, try not to be too down about it. At least you've still got Zach.'

Elsa gave a wan smile. 'I'd better get on. It's busy today. I think it's because it's so cold outside, everyone wants warming up.'

On Thursday morning, as Katy was doing an extra shift at the café, Elsa decided it was time she put her skates on again. The session started quietly. She had the ice to herself for about fifteen minutes, then noticed a skater with ice hockey skates had come on.

Concentrating on doing half circles on the outside edges of her blades, she heard the sound of quick strokes as the ice hockey skater came up behind her. Suddenly she felt a strong blow between her shoulder blades, and she went down like a stone, slamming into the hard surface. She gave an exclamation of dismay and pain. The figure loomed over her, and gripped her shoulder. But instead of lifting her up and apologising, she heard the hissed words in her ear, 'Keep your nose out from where you're not wanted!'

Winded, she lay there trying to get her breath and calm her thumping heart. Her knees stung, and her elbow was sore. After about a minute she thought that she would be able to try and stand up. Then she became aware of another figure at her side. Looking up, she saw the concerned face of an elderly man with thinning grey hair.

'Are you all right? Are you hurt?'

He was wearing ordinary shoes, like all the maintenance staff who took a short cut across the ice.

'I — I'm not sure.' Elsa's limbs felt weak with shock.

'Here, let me help you up.' His arms were strong as he pulled her to her feet. She was wearing leggings, so didn't think she had broken the skin on her knees, but they were very sore as she limped to the gate and crumpled on to one of the seats.

'Trying something difficult, were you?' he said kindly, obviously attempting to console her.

'No, I wasn't, I was just practising my edges.' Her breath was ragged as she tried not to cry with shock. 'It was another skater, he bashed into me and knocked me down.'

The elderly man looked round the rink in bewilderment. 'But there's nobody else here. Are you sure?'

'Of course I'm sure!' She lifted her head and looked him in the eye. 'I couldn't possibly have fallen as hard as I did, doing slow edges.' Pulling up her sleeve, she examined her left elbow, which was scraped by the fabric of her jumper. 'He — he said I should keep my nose out where I wasn't wanted.' She took a ragged breath, holding back a sob.

He shook his head with a bemused look. 'I don't see how anyone could have got off the ice so quickly. There was no one here when I arrived.'

Elsa didn't know what was worse

— falling on the ice or not being believed.

'I've been here all my working life, and I've never known anyone be attacked on the ice,' he said.

A thought crossed Elsa's mind. 'Excuse me, but are you Pete, Gina's husband?'

'Yes, I am.' He looked puzzled.

'I'm Elsa, from the Rainbow Café. Gina said that you had been working here since you were young.'

'I have — and I've never regretted it.'

Elsa rubbed her arms. She was beginning to feel cold, though her strength was coming back. 'I think I'll just pack up my things and go home. Please don't tell anyone what I said about another skater. I'll just tell Jean that I had a tumble and decided to give up for today.'

'Well, that's probably best. After all, no one else saw the mysterious skater.'

Elsa couldn't understand how Pete had missed the man on ice hockey skates. Unless, of course, he had gone straight into one of the storerooms, or upstairs.

Limping home, a sick dread filled her as she mulled over how Daniel had told her that all these sinister happenings could just be a coincidence. Maybe Arnie had indeed committed suicide. Perhaps there was a rougher element coming to the ice rink. Or maybe Daniel himself was involved and didn't want her asking questions. After all, he'd been with Arnie on the night he died. He could have had the opportunity to put sleeping pills in the whisky, knowing that no one would come to the office once the competition was over. Was Daniel so ruthless in wanting to take over the rink that he could commit murder? The two thugs who had attacked Zach could have been in Daniel's pay. After all, he had arranged for all the renovation work. If there was something shady going on, it would be easy enough to bring in criminals under the guise of being workmen. Plus, she remembered how Daniel had skated with her that day earlier in the year. He knew that she sometimes came to a quiet public session. He only had to wait for the opportunity to find her on her own, and he could so easily have been the tall figure on ice hockey skates. Opening up to him about her fears and suspicions could have spurred him to act.

Had he changed so much from the boy she had known?

Lisa took one look at her when she entered the café and hurried over to her, frowning. 'Elsa, what happened?'

Elsa began to shake again, so as the café was empty, Lisa helped her upstairs to her flat while she explained about her fall. She said nothing about the mysterious skater. It was only when she caught sight of herself in the mirror above the fireplace that she gasped. Her hair was tumbling down, and there was a red scrape on the right side of her face. 'I didn't realise that I looked so awful.'

'Sit down, I'll fetch something to bathe your face.'

Once she had explained to Lisa where she could find cotton wool and antiseptic, Elsa leaned back in her chair and stroked Missy, who had jumped up beside her. The little cat soon tucked herself in the corner between the arm of the easy chair and her mistress's hip, which was very comforting. Elsa closed her eyes and let Lisa bathe her face, which was beginning to sting. She also let her treat her elbow, and they examined her knees.

'They're just bruised, I think. It's a dangerous sport, ice skating.' Lisa tutted. 'I'm sticking to the gym.'

Elsa hadn't the strength to argue. Luckily, Lisa was happy to work in the café for the rest of the day, so she didn't have to show her face. Lisa even did the cleaning after closing time and brought up a sandwich from the leftovers before she went home. Elsa curled up on the settee with Missy for the evening.

Natalie came into the café again on Sunday after the class. 'This is beginning to become a habit,' she scolded as she collected a cupcake and a coffee. 'You'll have me putting on weight if you don't come to class every week. Look at you! Practising something hard, I suppose.'

'Yes.' Elsa decided just to go along with this explanation. The alternative seemed to be ridiculous, and the more she thought about it, the more she wondered if it was in fact a figment of her imagination. Maybe the skater had just knocked her by mistake, and was too cowardly to apologise?

'We finished the steps for the Christmas routine today. Do you want to come skating with me on Tuesday evening, and I'll show it to you?'

'Thanks, that would be great. Sorry, I must go, Natalie. It's very busy today. Are you going for six o'clock?'

'Yes, I'll grab a sandwich as I leave work.'

Elsa was glad to escape, knowing that

Natalie had a knack of wheedling the truth out of her. If she was honest, she didn't feel much like going skating again for a while. She didn't know who she had upset, but that gruff, threatening voice had frightened her.

Waking on Tuesday morning, Elsa's throat and head hurt, so it was a good excuse to text Natalie and pull out of their skating session. Feeling miserable, she staggered downstairs and began baking. At least she had plenty to keep her busy.

Lisa called in sick the next day, sounding very croaky on the telephone. 'I'm sorry, I really feel terrible. I know you've got a cold, too, but I can hardly lift my head off the pillow.'

Elsa, who was feeling very hot, put a hand to her forehead. 'No, don't worry. Stay in bed, I'll manage.' It was only after she had put down the receiver that she realised that Katy was unavailable this week, because she had university exams.

It felt like the longest day of her life.

Her legs were like lead by the afternoon. She hoped that she wasn't passing on any germs to her customers, doing her best to sneeze out of sight, and washing her hands frequently. Her voice was fast disappearing, too.

'I was wondering what had happened to you.' The voice came to her as if through a long tunnel. Elsa looked up from the coffee machine, where she was making two cappuccinos for customers, to see Daniel's concerned face on the other side of the counter.

'You don't look well.'

'Well, thanks, Daniel. That makes me feel a lot better.' Her voice was little more than a croak.

'I've been away for the past week, and when I came back, I heard about your fall at the ice rink. I was worried that you hadn't been in since then. But now I'm even more worried. You shouldn't be at work.'

'Lisa's got flu, and Katy has exams, so there's no one else to run the café. We can't close, as people won't come back.' Her eyes immediately went to the clock, and saw that it was half past four.

'I think you're closing early today.' He turned and walked to the door, flipping the 'Open' sign round.

Elsa hadn't the strength to protest. In fact, it was a relief to have someone take over and make decisions. He took a tray and helped her clear the tables. The last two customers left at quarter to five, so Daniel pulled down the blinds. When she reached for the cleaning materials, he took them from her hands.

'You sit down, and tell me what to wipe.'

The look of surprise on her face made him smile. 'I'm used to looking after myself, you know. My mother trained me well.'

Her head thumping, Elsa could only watch gratefully while he briskly wiped the tables. Then he shooed her upstairs while he loaded the dishwasher and set it going. 'Put your pyjamas on — you need to get to bed.'

She emerged from the bathroom in her dressing gown and slippers, to find him trying to coax Missy on to his lap. 'She's a one-person cat. Maybe if you give her some treats she'll look upon you more favourably.'

Daniel went into the kitchen and after a few minutes returned with a hot medicated drink for her, and a packet of cat treats. He laughed when Missy jumped down from the settee and began rubbing round his ankles, purring. 'Well, I think I've made a conquest.' The cat daintily crunched the treats when he tossed them one at a time on the carpet.

Elsa closed her eyes as she sipped the hot drink, letting the warmth course through her body and finding that she could breathe better. She had been feeling shivery for several hours. It was comforting to have Daniel pulling the curtains and seeing to Missy. He gave the cat her supper, then returned to Elsa, who was sitting on the settee still cradling her mug.

He took it from her hands and laid it on the table, then sat beside her and pulled her into the crook of his arm. He said nothing, for which she was glad, as her throat felt too sore to speak. With a sigh, she rested her head on his shoulder. He bent down and kissed her forehead briefly, before holding her tightly against him. Missy crept into the little space at Elsa's side, and soon she drifted off to sleep.

# 12

Elsa woke in the middle of the night to find herself in bed, but once she had registered this sensation, just turned over and slept. The sensation of a cat jumping on the bed roused her eventually. Through a crack in the curtains she could see blue sky, and when she turned towards her alarm clock the hands were almost at ten o'clock. In horror, she staggered out of bed, let Missy out, then dragged herself into the bathroom. The face reflected back in the mirror looked terrible, all puffy, and as she gazed at it in dismay, she gave a deep rattling cough. Oh, no, there was no way she could work today. In misery, she pulled on her dressing gown and booted up her computer. She printed off a notice, to say that the café would be closed all day. She didn't think that Lisa would be back for a few days, either. Then she slipped downstairs to tape it to the door.

Searching in her bathroom cabinet, she found a box with three more sachets of cold remedy, so boiled the kettle and made up a mug. In the meantime, Missy had returned, so she put down a bowl of fresh cat food and a plate of biscuits, and changed her water. Once Elsa had finished her drink, she returned to her bedroom, put the radio on low, and drifted in and out of sleep for the rest of the morning.

By late afternoon, she was eating a small bowl of soup when the doorbell to the flat chimed. Elsa was tempted to ignore it, but after it rang again, she groaned and pulled a thick jumper over her pyjamas. Missy ran down the stairs in front of her. Opening the door a crack, she was astonished and gratified to find Daniel's tall frame filling the doorway. A cold gust of wind blew some dry leaves in the door.

'May I come in? I wanted to make sure that you were all right.'

He followed her back up to the flat. Her legs felt heavy as she climbed the stairs, and flopped on to the settee. Sitting in the chair opposite her, he placed a plastic carrier bag on the coffee table. Missy jumped up and poked her nose into it, at which they both laughed, though Elsa's dissolved into a coughing fit.

'That doesn't sound too good. I see you didn't open the café today. Is your assistant still off?'

She nodded. 'I couldn't face opening.' Her voice was just a croak.

'I brought you some supplies — I noticed that you didn't have much in the bathroom cabinet. I bought some of the same brand that you have, plus some herbal cough lozenges and a jar of honey. My mother swears by it, though I prefer it with a tot of whisky.'

Touched by his concern, she smiled, thanking him.

'Have you plenty to eat? I can go to the corner shop if you need anything like bread or milk.'

Giving a shaky grin, she shook her head. 'Daniel, this is a café — I have a freezer full of supplies, including bread buns, loaves of bread, plus frozen soup and cakes. Then I have my own food up here in the flat. Don't worry, I'm fine.'

His face registered concern. 'Well, if you're sure. I would cook you a meal if you like.'

'I'm managing.' She gestured towards the soup bowl on the kitchen table. 'I've been sleeping most of the day, and I'll watch some television this evening and have an early night.' She gave a deep cough. 'Thanks for the medicines — I really appreciate it.'

'Well, then, I'd better go, as you're clearly not up to visitors yet.' He stood up, hovering for a moment as if reluctant to leave. 'I'll see myself out.'

Elsa leaned back and closed her eyes. If she didn't feel so lousy, she would have been delighted. Instead, she just pulled her dressing gown back on and opened a packet of throat lozenges from the supplies that Daniel had left on the table. Then she picked up the remote control for the television.

It was Saturday before she managed to open the café again. Her mother had telephoned that morning to find out how she was, and insisted on coming along to help her out.

'But you've been at work all week. I can't have you spending your weekend with me.'

'Rubbish! I'd feel much worse thinking of you struggling with the café on your own. I helped out when you started up, remember. I did my weekend shopping last night after work, so I can be there for opening time. Do you need me to pick anything up for you on the way?'

'No, thanks. You're a gem.' She hadn't told her mother about Daniel's visit, and all the cold remedies. She smiled as she put the phone down. He had telephoned her every day to see how she was. It was nice to have all this attention.

Elsa insisted that she would manage

on her own on Sunday, but of course it meant missing her skating class again. At eleven o'clock, Natalie arrived at the café, her concern hidden behind a grumbling façade, complaining that Elsa was determined to make her waistline expand. Still, it didn't stop her tucking into her usual pink cupcake and coffee. She stopped behind and cleared some tables for Elsa, and loaded the dishwasher with the morning's crockery. Elsa closed at four o'clock on Sundays in winter, but as it was a grim day it was growing dark soon after three, and there were no customers in the café.

'I think I'll close up before anyone else arrives,' she told Natalie, who had just finished wiping the last of the tables.

As Elsa went to flip the sign, she found Daniel approaching the door. Natalie's eyebrows rose when Elsa let him in.

'How are you feeling, Elsa? How have you managed today?'

She smiled. 'It's not been too busy, and Natalie kindly helped after skating class.'

Natalie untied the apron she had borrowed and laid it on the counter. 'Well, you provided me with a free lunch, so I've been well paid. Now, I think it's time I was getting home to Mark.'

'Thanks, Natalie. You've been marvellous. I really appreciate it.'

'I'll expect free coffee and cakes for the next two months, and then a course at Weight Watchers to lose it all again,' she joked as she grabbed her coat. On reaching the door, she gave her friend a quick hug, and smiled briefly at Daniel before leaving the café.

Elsa pulled down the blinds and offered Daniel a coffee. 'There's plenty of cake left as well. I'll pop it in the freezer if you don't want it.'

'Let me help,' he insisted. 'I can't have you waiting on me.' He soon silenced her protests, as fatigue was threatening to overcome her, and she had begun coughing again. He put the final load in the dishwasher while Elsa put the leftover cake in containers and stacked them in the freezer. She kept out a couple of pieces of fruit cake for them, which they took upstairs to the flat.

Daniel insisted on making their drinks, and settled down next to her on the settee. Missy rubbed round their legs until she was given some biscuits. They sat in silence for a while, just listening to the gentle crunching of the cat eating. Missy then jumped up on to the windowsill to look out, her tail twitching.

'It's the wind in the trees; she loves watching the movement.' Elsa laid her mug on the table and leaned back, sighing. 'Oh, that's good.'

'I'm not staying long. I only called in to see how you were. I'm going to my brother Andrew's house for a meal.'

She felt both disappointed and relieved, because she was longing to stretch out on her bed. 'How's Poppy?

Still enjoying her skating?'

He laughed. 'Very excited about the Christmas show. She has to have a fairy costume for her class's contribution. There's one little boy in the group, and he'll be an elf.'

'Oh to be seven again!' Then she became serious. 'I don't know whether I'm going to be in our performance now. I've missed so much, and to be honest, I don't know when I'll be back skating.'

Daniel turned to look at her. 'I'm sorry to hear that. Irina told me she thought that you were doing really well, developing a nice flow in your skating.'

Tightness gripped her heart at the mention of the Russian coach. 'I'm surprised she's so relaxed about you spending so much time with me this past week. Is she going with you to your brother's?'

His forehead creased. 'Irina? We've had a few meetings about the Christmas show and our progress in bringing the Ice Stars next summer. We think they can fit us in on the end of their tour, before they go back to London for their finale. But I certainly wouldn't be seeing her on a Sunday, as she'll be wanting to spend that with her little boy. She barely knows my brother. Why would you think . . . ?'

'I . . . I just assumed, as you were together . . . You *are* seeing her, aren't you?' Elsa's heart was racing.

He looked perplexed. 'No, not now. We did have a fling soon after I split with Hannah, but after a few months we realised that there was nothing lasting in our relationship. I admire her very much for her talents, and for her devotion as a mother, but she's really too driven for me. I see her as a different version of Hannah.'

Elsa felt as if she was slipping on the ice again. If Daniel wasn't with Irina, was it significant that he was lavishing all this attention on her — or was he just being a kind friend?

Her thoughts were interrupted when the telephone shrilled, making her jump. Daniel stood up. 'I'd better go. I'll be in touch soon. Take care, now.'

'Thanks,' she mumbled, reaching for the telephone. It was her mother, concerned about how she had managed. For a few moments she only answered automatically, watching Daniel as he shrugged into his fleece and waved at her. Something inside her was melting, especially when he gave Missy a tickle under her chin on his way out.

Monday was the first real day off she had had for many weeks, but she felt listless. She went for a short walk along the seafront, and found that her legs were feeling stronger. Her cough was less rattly, and by the afternoon she was beginning to think about baking again, and made a lemon drizzle cake for the next day.

By Thursday she was feeling much better, especially as Lisa and Katy had returned to work, so she phoned Natalie at lunchtime to see if she would come skating after work. 'Do you think there's still time for me to learn the routine for the Christmas show?'

'Of course! And it's time you started thinking about a costume. As it's *Cabaret*, we're all talking of wearing black Lycra shorts with fishnet tights. Fiona's sourcing some cheap black bowler hats on the internet. You can text her if you want one.'

Elsa's hesitations began to dissolve, especially once she was back on her skates with Natalie. After a few rounds on the ice, she was finding her legs again, and they worked through the routine for the next hour. Tired, but not exhausted, that night she slept better than she had done for a long time.

A week later, they were queuing at the ice rink with a throng of little girls in sparkling dresses and Christmas costumes, little boys dressed as elves and even a snowman and a Santa Claus. The noise level was almost unbearable, as the children shrieked with laughter and shouted at each other excitedly over the hubbub. It was

Saturday lunchtime, and Christmas was almost upon them. Elsa had left Lisa in charge at the café, and had walked round to the ice rink with a long coat over her costume.

'You're changed already!' Natalie had accused her. 'I brought my stuff with me. Come on, we've been told that the adults can use the changing rooms.'

'This is just an excuse to see how they've been done up.' Elsa followed her, taking care not to bash her plastic bowler hat in the crowd. Daniel had texted that he was looking forward to seeing her at the show, and was sorry he hadn't contacted her as he'd been away again on business. The excitement she was already feeling about the show was doubled by anticipation of seeing him again. Were they going to rekindle their relationship? The thought was a background theme to all of her actions.

They turned down the corridor to the right of the box office, and opened the dressing room door. Fiona and two of the other adults were there, as well as two of the coaches and Bethany. Elsa watched through the corner of her eyes as the young skater prepared her costume. It was truly spectacular — she was to be the Ice Queen (Elsa had wondered mischievously if that was typecasting). A sparkling white sleeveless skating dress had been accessorised with cascading silver and white ribbons from the shoulders, and a fan of wider ribbons trailing like icicles from the back of the skirt. The young woman was making up her face with dramatic make-up, dark eyes and silver glitter tracking from her eyes towards her temples. To finish it off, she placed a sparking tiara with long points on her blonde hair, which had been put up into a bun. Around this she twisted more ribbons, letting a few fall down to her neck. It was a stunning effect.

As Bethany was getting ready, Tara Fitzsimmons entered. Her eyes immediately flickered to the older girl, and she headed to the opposite end of the dressing table. The adult skaters were checking each other's costumes, especially their bow ties and hats, so they weren't focused on Tara. Suddenly there was a scream, and the girl leaped back, a piece of paper in her hand. With horror, she shook it from her fingers and burst into tears.

'Tara, what's wrong?' Wendy, one of the coaches, rushed over to her.

At first the girl could only sob, but finally managed to say, 'That — that was in the top of my trolley!'

Wendy bent to retrieve the piece of paper that Tara had dropped on the floor. The other adults moved over, and Elsa could see the writing on the note that the coach was holding in her hand. It had been handwritten in blood-red capital letters. *'Today you will die like your grandfather.'*

# 13

'It's just some silly prank,' Wendy stated firmly. Elsa admired her calm and presence of mind.

'But how did it get there?' Tara wailed, covering her face with her hands.

'Well, none of us put it in — it must have been there before you got here.' Bethany finished putting a sequin on her cheek, and turned to them, her face bland. She was the only one in the dressing room who seemed unconcerned.

Everyone else looked at each other. What Bethany said was true. But what was clearly in everyone's minds (except Bethany's) was that they had a show to put on, and if Tara was in a state, and not able to skate, it could flounder, as she had several important roles.

Wendy persuaded Tara to sit down,

an arm around the girl's shoulder. 'I wouldn't take it seriously. Anyone could have slipped it in for a sick joke, as you don't look at your bag all the time.'

'But what if it's *true*?'

Elsa reached into her bag for a bottle of water and broke the seal on it. 'Of course it isn't! Here, have a sip. This will help calm you down.'

'I'm sure that *no one* wishes you ill.' Fiona came to stand by her shoulder.

'But Granddad died, didn't he — someone killed him! My gran said that he would never have committed suicide.'

A stab of shock ran through Elsa at this resurrection of her old suspicions, while the others exclaimed in dismay, 'No, that's not true. The result of the inquest didn't prove that.' No matter what the truth was about Arnie, Elsa couldn't believe that anyone would want to hurt Tara.

Bethany stood up. 'I shall have to go. I'm starting off the show, and they'll have finished preparing the ice, so I'd better be ready.'

Once she had gone, Tara said bitterly, 'How can she be so calm? I bet she was the one to put it in my bag!'

Relieved that Tara was beginning to think of the incident as a prank, Elsa took back the water. 'Well, if that's the case, you need to show her that she's not going to beat you down.'

'Elsa's right.' Wendy lifted Tara's red sequinned dress from its cover, and shook it out. 'Come on, time to get ready.' Handing the girl a tissue with a smile, she was rewarded with a watery smile in return. Soon Tara looked resplendent, and Fiona helped her with her make-up as her hands were shaking.

'Now, deep breaths. Let's do a warm-up.' Wendy nodded her thanks to the others as they left, taking their coats to keep them warm while they waited for their turn.

'We're on quite early,' Natalie said as they walked down the corridor on their skate blade guards. 'Item number twelve.'

'Good, then we can sit back and enjoy the rest of the show.' Elsa's gaze flickered round the throngs of children with their parents, looking for Daniel. Some of the performers were grouped round their coaches who were either giving them a warm-up or just going through steps with them. The entrances to the rink and the cafeteria observation windows were covered with heavy blackout curtains so they couldn't see through.

Fiona examined the programme pinned up beside the main entrance by the skate hire. Before she could read it properly, she was elbowed aside by Bethany, who pulled back the blackout curtain and opened the door. Several little girls gazed in admiration at her dazzling appearance, but the haughty features were turned solely towards the ice rink, with no acknowledgement of their adoration.

Irina was at her elbow. 'The ice is prepared now. Are you ready?'

With a toss of her tiara-crowned

head, Bethany gave a terse 'Yes' before stepping through the curtain, followed by Irina. Elsa, Natalie and Fiona slipped through behind her, pulling their coats closer to combat the chill of the rink area. They ascended the nearest rank of seats, high enough to see over the Perspex ice-hockey shielding that permanently surrounded the ice. The surfacing machine was being driven into the well in the back centre, leaving the ice shining and smooth.

Within moments there was a recorded fanfare, followed by Carl Fitzsimmons's voice booming over the loudspeaker. 'Ladies and gentlemen, welcome to Heronsburn Ice Rink Christmas Show. Let the festivity begin!' His words were followed by a swirl of music, and Bethany powered her way across the ice, immediately going into her programme. It was breathtakingly impressive — turns, curves, effortless leaps, finishing with a spin so fast she became a blur before their eyes. A roar of appreciation greeted her final pose.

After watching the first few acts, the three women descended the stairs to join the rest of their group in the area beside the vending machines. They discarded their coats and put on their bowler hats. Natalie grabbed her phone and asked a parent standing by to take their photo. Elsa was waiting to hand over her own, when she heard a deep voice at her side.

'Shall I do the honours?'

Whirling round, she found Daniel holding out his hand. Her heart gave a great bound as she handed over her phone. 'Come on, in line again!' she called to the others, trying to appear nonchalant. They all struck a pose.

'Good luck!' he said. 'You all look fabulous. I'm looking forward to this.'

'Don't look forward too much,' said Netta, a small black woman in her thirties. 'You might find it's a comedy number rather than a jazzy one!'

They all laughed, on the edge of hysteria with nerves, but Elsa felt excited at the prospect of performing. Natalie added, 'Well, at least it'll be entertaining.'

Laura, their coach, beckoned them to go to the tunnel. Here they had a chilly wait before they emerged on to the ice. Elsa's heart began to pound, but she remembered from her childhood dancing days to plaster a smile on her face and keep it there no matter what. They were in position, and the music began. Daniel was forgotten as she followed through her steps, keeping up with the others. Although the performance was several minutes long, it seemed to be over in the blink of an eye, and they were skating off the ice to ringing applause.

'Whew! I didn't fall over, though I nearly lost my balance when we were skating off.' Natalie took off her bowler hat and shook her hair out as soon as they were off the ice. 'My throat's parched. Let's grab a drink and watch the rest.'

They climbed back up to the seats

they had occupied earlier, euphoric at their success. 'When's Tara on?' Natalie took a swig of her water.

'Fiona has a programme.' They reached over to borrow it from her. 'Number thirty-one — she's doing a number with Jacob. We're on sixteen at the moment. Do you think Wendy managed to persuaded her to skate?'

'I hope so. It would be a tragedy if she didn't. Especially after Bethany doing so well. She needs to hold up the Heronsburn honour.'

They sat through a mixed bag of performances. Two of the girls fell over during their programmes, which weren't that interesting anyway. Then a little boy came on and wowed them all with his snowman routine. Two of the older girls did a comedy routine of Laurel and Hardy, which received enthusiastic applause.

Item thirty-one approached, and Carl announced Tara and Jacob. They skated confidently out from the well, holding hands. Then their music began, and while Natalie and Elsa held their breath, they skated a most beautiful programme. There was a great deal of synchronised skating, including jumps, as well as lifts, and towards the end he swung her right up over his head, where she was poised for over ten seconds. Applause and cheers rippled round the rink. When they dipped into their final pose, the audience erupted, including the little group of adult performers, who whooped and cheered.

'She did it! What a trouper!' Elsa took off her gloves so that she could clap loudly.

'That'll show 'em!' Natalie exclaimed.

As the couple came off the ice at the gate below them, Irina and Wendy were waiting to hug and congratulate them. But once they had moved past, Tara's head lowered and she was clearly in tears. They saw Jacob's arm come round her, holding her close against him, and he bent to kiss the top of her head.

Elsa and turned to Natalie. 'Well! If it

was Bethany doing that prank out of jealousy, I think her plan misfired. It looks as if this has brought out something between Tara and Jacob.'

'Do you think Bethany's after him?'

'From what I've heard, she followed *him* here, not Irina. I knew that Tara liked him, but it looks as if it's reciprocated.'

'Good!' Natalie put her gloves back on.

At that moment, Daniel came up the stairs and slipped into the seat beside Elsa. 'Well done! Your *Cabaret* number was brilliant.'

'Laura will be pleased to hear that,' Natalie said.

'I wasn't looking at anyone else, just keeping my mind on my own part.' Elsa smiled at him, glad that he was relaxed enough to come and speak with her when she was with her friends.

'One or two people have commented about how good it was. A very good advert for our adult skating programme.'

'Is that all we are? An advert?' Fiona laughed.

'Well, I can't deny that it might encourage others to start, but you made a very tasteful addition to the show. We've never had so many adults skating, and we're keen to encourage it.'

Conversation drifted as the ice show continued. Daniel spoke more quietly, for Elsa's benefit. 'I heard about the incident with Tara. You were there, weren't you?' When she nodded, he went on, 'I don't suppose you have any idea how anyone could have reached her bag?'

'I don't know. We were all involved in our own costumes at the time. Although Bethany seems the most likely culprit, she was at the mirror doing her make-up. Do you think the threat could be real?'

Daniel frowned. 'I can't believe that anyone could wish her ill — but I'll keep my eyes open. Her father, Carl, has been told, too.'

'I'm pleased she was able to perform.

She was marvellous.'

'Yes, that girl's going to go far. She's come on so much since starting to train with Irina. To perform like that after such an upset shows that she's really got something. I believe that she and Jacob could make a future as a pair skating duo.'

Mischievously, Elsa said, 'Are they a pair in more than one way? They seemed very close when they left the ice.'

He grinned. 'You're a real romantic, aren't you? Although I must confess that I thought the same thing when I saw them — they were holding hands.'

'Bethany's nose will be truly out of joint.'

A smile passed between them. 'I'd better go,' he said finally. 'I'll be in touch later.'

'A lot of our group is going out tonight in town.'

'Okay then, tomorrow. See you soon.' He squeezed her shoulder as he left.

Natalie turned her head. 'He'll be in

touch later? Is this becoming serious?' Her eyes were dancing.

Elsa hugged herself beneath her coat, unable to hide the joy in her face. 'I'm not sure — but I hope so.'

'Poor Zach. He'll have to go on the hunt again.' Despite her words, Natalie didn't look stern.

'I'm sorry — I never felt more than friendship for him. Maybe he'll find a nice Australian woman.'

'I hope not! He's not moving out there!'

Six of their group met up in the pub at the end of the promenade on the seafront later that evening, including Elsa, Natalie and Fiona. Relief and euphoria made them throw inhibitions to the wind, and the wine flowed freely.

Inevitably they spent much of the evening discussing the events earlier in the day.

'The show has really shown Irina in a different light,' Natalie said while she and Elsa shuffled into a banquette seat. 'It was lovely to see her little boy,

Dmitri, on the ice in his wheelchair.'

Some of the coaches, including Irina, had performed a routine to *The Fairytale of New York*. In the closing moments of the song, two of the male coaches had pushed him onto the ice. Dressed in a red jumper and Santa hat, the little boy had waved his hands in delight as they pushed him across the ice, while a huge cheer erupted from the audience.

'He had such a big grin on his little face at his mother's surprise' Fiona remarked.

Alex, one of the male coaches, had caught the handles of the chair and spun it round, while the other coaches skated around it.

'I loved the way that they finished in a picture pose with Dmitri in the centre, as if it was all rehearsed. No wonder the audience clapped so hard'. Elsa smiled at the memory as she swirled her white wine in its glass.

'I think everyone was moved, especially as he was obviously enjoying himself.' Natalie took a sip of her red wine. 'They didn't realise that she had a disabled child.'

'He's absolutely adorable!' Elsa had been surprised at how touched she had been by the sight of the Russian coach with her son, especially later, holding his hand and waving with him at her students when they were leaving. She was seeing Irina's softer side, and could understand how Daniel had been attracted to her — but thankfully no more. There was a tiny bubble of excitement within her every time she thought of his promise to ring her.

It turned out to be a late night. Elsa decided to give skating class a miss on the Sunday morning, knowing that she had to work, and her head was rather thick after the amount of wine they had consumed. As the day went by and there was nothing from Daniel, she told herself sternly not to mind.

It was after nine o'clock, and she had almost given up, when the longed-for call finally came. Her stomach fluttered as his voice sounded in her ear. They chatted about the ice show and her night out. His next words took her breath away. 'Elsa, I've been invited to a local Chamber of Commerce Christmas do, and wondered if you'd like to come with me as my guest.'

Stunned for a moment, with delicious visions of evening dresses and black ties, Elsa paused. 'I — I'm not a member of the Chamber of Commerce.'

She could tell from his voice that he was smiling. 'You don't have to be, to come as my guest — but I'll enjoy introducing you as a successful businesswoman. Did that article ever appear in the newspaper?'

Snapping out of her reverie, she replied, 'Yes, my mother found it in the local paper about three weeks ago. Nathan Troutbeck was genuine after all. Have you heard anything from him?'

'No.' There was a momentary pause before he continued. 'The event is next Wednesday, at the Heronsburn Manor

Hotel. I'm looking forward to seeing you in a posh frock. I'll call you again with the timings.'

He rang off, leaving Elsa stunned and excited. This surely was a proper date. Did this mean that they were back together again, after all these years?

# 14

'What am I going to wear? I've nothing that's remotely suitable for a black-tie dinner, and I can't afford to buy something new.' On Monday night Elsa was ringing Natalie in a panic, having raked through her wardrobe.

'Let me think . . . You're the same dress size as me, even though you're a bit taller. I have a dress that I bought on a whim last year for Mark's sister's wedding, but changed my mind. Why not come round tomorrow and try it on?'

They agreed that Elsa would pick up a takeaway meal from the Chinese restaurant on the seafront to take to Natalie's house. Once they had eaten, and Mark was spreading out some of his pupils' books on the kitchen table to do a bout of marking, the two women repaired upstairs to the couple's bedroom.

'Natalie! You've been decorating. This is gorgeous!' Elsa looked round the room in admiration.

Natalie stroked the purple and gold cushions that matched the bedspread and curtains. 'I adore it — quite the harem effect, don't you think?' A gold chiffon curtain was draped from the ceiling to the purple headboard. The carpet was pale gold, the walls papered in a colour somewhere between gold and buttermilk. There was a new print above the bed, a giant purple flower on a plain background.

'I'm so envious! You're giving me ideas.'

'Better get decorating, then. You need a romantic bedroom now — some action is in sight.'

Elsa slapped her friend with the other cushion. 'Behave, Mrs. Bates. Act your age!' But she couldn't hide a self-conscious grin.

'Well, we must subdue our carnal thoughts and knuckle down to work.'

Natalie slid back the wardrobe door and began rummaging through her clothes. 'There! That's what I was looking for.' She brought out a sliver of dark green silk on a hanger and held it up against Elsa.

Elsa caught the edge of the dress, sleeveless and cut on the bias, and looked in the mirrored door as she held it against her. It came to just above her knee.

'I knew it!' Natalie said. 'That colour's great on you. It didn't suit me at all. What do you think?'

'I adore it.' It was like a deep sea pool, the silk shimmering in the light as Elsa swayed from side to side. Within a few minutes she had shed her clothes and had slipped the cool silk over her head. The dress fell into place with a whisper. The two women scrutinized Elsa's reflection.

'It'll be perfect with a pair of heels. Try these.' Natalie placed a pair of black platform shoes in front of her.

With a grimace, Elsa squeezed her

feet into them. 'They're a size too small, but I suppose it gives the effect. Wow!' It was true. The extra height of the heels was ideal for the length of the dress.

The following night, Elsa surveyed herself in her own mirror, wearing the dress. On her feet were her own black patent high-heeled shoes. Natalie had lent her the green silk clutch bag that went with the outfit, and Elsa had a black velvet coat to put on top, plus a large black pashmina scarf. Her hair was twisted on top of her head, with several curls pulled out on each side to frame her face. Her make-up was more dramatic than usual, with darker eyeliner and mascara, and a new lipstick and nail varnish, something she seldom wore because of all her baking.

When Daniel arrived she was wearing her coat, so he didn't get the full effect of her outfit until they handed in their outer wear at the cloakroom in the hotel. Turning back to him, her pashmina over her shoulder, she heard him give a low whistle. 'Beautiful! I knew you would look stunning.'

His admiration gave her a warm glow. 'You're looking quite amazing yourself,' she replied. *What is it about a man in a tuxedo?* she thought. It outlined the width of his shoulders, and made him look even taller. The perfect white of his shirt and the neat bow tie gave him the appearance of a film star. His hair was beginning to spring out of the style he had combed it into before he had left home, which made him look boyish and appealing. Just looking at him made her feel weak at the knees.

The touch of his hand on her bare back sent a shiver of attraction through her as they made their way into the reception room. Comparing herself with the other guests (mostly older than the two of them), she began to feel less nervous and satisfied that she didn't look out of place.

'Good to see you, Daniel! And who is this?' The greeting came from a short man with a shock of grey hair, his stomach bulging slightly beneath his shirt. His expression was open and welcoming.

'Jeremy, let me introduce Elsa Turnfield, proprietor of the Rainbow Café in Heronsburn. Elsa, this is Jeremy Nicholls, my solicitor. We've been seeing rather a lot of each other recently.'

Elsa took the hand that Nicholls held out to her, and he shook it warmly. 'Ah, yes, I've seen your café. The previous proprietors let it get very run down. You've done a marvellous job with it. I must tell my wife to call in sometime; it looks very inviting.'

Elsa thanked him, feeling more confident, believing she really had a right to be there. Shortly after, when Daniel was in conversation with another of his contacts, Elsa found herself talking with a couple of businesswomen who ran a jeweller's shop in the area. 'It belonged to our father, but once he died our brother wasn't interested in retail, so we took it over. That was ten years ago, and we're doing fine.'

'Are there many other business-women here? I thought that it would be mostly men with their wives.'

'We're massively outnumbered.' The taller of the two women placed her empty wine glass on the tray of a passing waiter and took a full one to replace it. 'But there are more of us every year. Many of the businesses that women run are still the traditional type, such as hairdressing and fashion, but increasing numbers are venturing into the male realms, and are making a go of it.'

The other sister pointed her glass towards the window. 'The young woman over there is on the board of a chain of menswear retailers, and the tall woman in the red dress is head of a bakery firm. There's also the older Italian woman over there — she has run the family restaurant chain since her husband died twenty years ago, leaving her with a young family. They're now grown up, and are running three restaurants in the area. You'll know them.' She mentioned a popular Italian restaurant chain, at which Elsa's eyes widened.

'I had no idea that a woman was at the head of it all.'

'Giovanna is a very shrewd business-woman. I'll take you to meet her later.'

After a while, Daniel returned, apologising for having abandoned her. 'I really had to speak with one or two people. I'm glad that you found someone to talk to.'

Amazingly buoyant, Elsa denied feeling bored. 'I've met a lot of other local businesswomen, and they've told me about a networking group I could join.' Excited, she showed him a business card. 'I'm going to their first meeting of the year, in January.'

'That's great! I thought you would find it interesting. The food should be good, too.' A gong sounded as he spoke.

Elsa enjoyed the meal, but found the man sitting on her other side rather condescending about her business. He looked down his nose when she mentioned that she ran a café, and turned to tell his wife, who smiled indulgently but was clearly not interested. After a rather limping conversation, she was glad when Daniel turned back to her.

They danced to the live band for a couple of hours, as well as chatting to some more people. It was almost midnight when people began to drift away. The band called the final number, so Elsa and Daniel joined the queue for their coats.

It was almost one o'clock when they passed the ice rink on the way to Elsa's place. They hadn't talked much on the way home, conversation drifting into tiredness as they neared the seafront. Elsa's mind was full of all the people she had met, plus the delight of sitting next to Daniel in his car, dressed in his dinner suit. Anticipation was flickering inside her, wondering how they would part — or if she should ask him in for a coffee.

Then she sat up with a start. 'Daniel, look, that's one of the lorries that I've seen before in the middle of the night. It's heading away from the ice rink, but it could well have turned out of the car park, don't you think?'

'I'm going to take a look.' He swerved into a bus stop layby, and did a U-turn. 'You don't mind, do you?'

She murmured her assent, her heart beginning to beat faster. The car park was empty, even round the back, where he parked the car. Tonight there were no sessions until the early patch at six in the morning. 'Stay here,' he said as he stepped out of the car. Elsa pulled her coat round her at the cold draught that blew in. It was only a few minutes before he returned. 'I can't see anything on the exterior, and there's no sign of forced entry. I'm going to take a quick look inside.'

'Daniel, are you sure? Don't you think we should call the police?'

'It seems a flimsy reason to call them

out — that we saw a large lorry near the ice rink. We didn't even see it come out from here. No, I'll slip in the small door at the rear and have a quiet snoop around. I always carry the key with me.'

Seeing his resolve, she let him go, but it didn't stop her worrying as the minutes ticked by. The cold began to seep into the car, so she pulled up the hood on her black velvet coat. At last she saw a movement at the door, and Daniel emerged again — but almost immediately she realised that it wasn't Daniel. Freezing in fear, she cowered in the corner of the passenger seat, as the shadowy figure looked round quickly and loped off into the darkness. Thank goodness he hadn't seen her in the car, with her black coat and hood.

But then she began to worry that the intruder might have attacked Daniel. How long should she wait before going in, or calling the police? Her patience had almost gone completely when the door opened again. The figure made straight for the car, and this time she recognised Daniel.

'I had a quick look round, taking care to be quiet, but there was no one there.' He slid into the seat beside her.

'But there was, Daniel. A man came out of the door after you went in — he must have heard you and slipped out before you saw him. Luckily he didn't notice me in the car. He must have thought you were here on your own.'

'Just one man?' He was alert again. 'I should go in and take another longer look. This isn't good.'

She grabbed his arm. 'What if there are more? They could attack you. I'll come with you.'

'No!' His response was immediate. 'You're right, it's foolish to go rooting around in the dark in these clothes.' He put his hand to his forehead. 'I heard rumours about strange happenings at the rink, but I thought that people were just seeing unfamiliar workmen for the renovations. This is more worrying.'

'Are you going to call the police?'

'There's so little to go on.' He started

the engine again, and eased the car out on to the deserted road. 'But I know now that something's going on, and I'll start looking round in earnest.'

They were silent on the way home, the golden atmosphere of the evening totally destroyed. Elsa's mind whirled with conflicting thoughts that she couldn't express out loud. How could Daniel not have suspected before that there was something sinister afoot at the ice rink? There had been so many incidents — including the mysterious male skater who had knocked her down several weeks ago. Of course, she had never mentioned that to him. Was now the time to do so?

When they pulled up outside Elsa's flat, he leaned over and kissed her lightly on the cheek. 'I hope you get some sleep, after all this.'

Giving him a wan smile, she thanked him for the dinner. 'I really did enjoy it, and I've made some useful contacts.' Then she ran over to her door and unlocked it. Now that the earlier euphoria had dampened, she almost felt like crying. The whole evening had been ruined.

At least Missy was waiting for her, curling round her legs and asking for attention. She picked up the cat and hugged her, though she wasn't a cuddly cat and soon began wriggling to be down. Elsa gave her some treats and boiled the kettle to make herself a drink. Despite her fatigue she wasn't ready for bed.

She almost dropped the kettle when the doorbell shrilled in the silence. Gingerly she made her way down the stairs, and put the chain on the door before opening it.

'I'm sorry, Elsa. Can I come in for a moment?' Daniel's expression was serious.

Undoing the chain, she opened the door, and as soon as he had closed it behind him, he gathered her in his arms and kissed her deeply. Responding avidly, she slid her arms up the fine wool of his jacket, feeling the stiff collar before her hands found his hair. The feel of his warm body against hers was like live electricity. The passion almost crackled between them as they tasted lips, kissed each other's faces and necks, breathing harshly as their hands roamed over each other's bodies. After a few minutes they finally separated reluctantly.

'I've been wanting to do that all evening, and I felt cheated when I let you go,' he murmured. 'That incident at the rink spoiled the whole mood of the evening. I couldn't let it ruin everything.'

'I did enjoy the evening — and being with you. Why not come up for a hot drink? I've just boiled the kettle.'

He drew away from her with a rueful expression. 'No, if I come up, I know that I'd find it hard to resist going further, and I'm afraid that my mind really isn't on romance now. I wouldn't want anything to spoil what we're rediscovering.'

Warmth spread through her at his

words. 'So are we back together?'

He brushed her lips briefly with his own. 'I'd like to start again — we've come a long way since we were teenagers, and I know that I'm a different person to that cocky boy who let you go all those years ago.'

'I'm willing to give it a go.' Why did she sound so calm when her whole being was singing? They melted into a final kiss, before he drew away.

'I'll call soon.'

# 15

They managed to meet only once more before Christmas was upon them and they had family commitments. Daniel was also doing a thorough search of the ice rink, though he confessed that he felt unable to confide in anyone else, as he didn't know who might be involved.

'This could have been going on before I arrived.'

'Tara said that Monica didn't believe Arnie would have taken his own life.'

'But don't you see, Elsa — if someone else put the pills in the drink, it would have to be a person that he knew and trusted. So it could be someone from the rink, or even his own family.'

'I can't believe that Carl or Robert could do that to their own father.'

'Me neither. But I need to go carefully. I hope that I haven't tipped them off by looking round that night — someone knows that I was there.'

On Christmas morning, Elsa's brother Jamie and his fiancée Louise came in their car to pick her up, as they were all going to their mother's house for the day.

'Mum told me that her guy, Graham, is coming over later,' she said as she and Jamie walked to the car. 'He's having Christmas dinner with his daughter and her family.'

'That's seriously weird,' Jamie replied. 'I can't imagine my mother having a boyfriend.' He frowned as he climbed into the driver's seat.

Elsa leaned over to hug Louise, a petite blonde with a wide smile, and they wished each other a happy Christmas.

Louise told them they were being unfair. 'You say he's a nice man — well, that's the best scenario. And if it makes your mum happy, that's ideal.'

'But what if — what if they want to get *married*?' Jamie turned the key in the ignition and moved off.

'I don't want a stepdad!' Elsa looked at her in horror.

Louise laughed at the expressions on their faces. 'That won't necessarily happen. Lots of older couples are in long-term relationships and never get married. They just like the companionship. You know that my parents divorced when I was a teenager, and they both have new partners. You'll get used to it.'

Elsa didn't mention that she suspected that Graham sometimes stayed over at their mum's house. She didn't want Jamie to be too freaked out before their meeting. He might just speak his mind before thinking and say something that could hurt their mum. It was a delicate situation.

It was good to be all together for the festive lunch. Elsa helped her mother with the final preparations, and managed to bring into the conversation her night out with Daniel.

Rachel turned to her with a quizzical

expression. 'So what does this mean? He seems very keen, to be taking you to a fancy dinner. Does this mean that it's back on?'

Elsa tried to appear nonchalant as she scooped roast potatoes into a serving dish. 'I think it is, Mum. But don't call it being 'back on'. This is nothing like that teenage romance. Daniel's a different person — and so am I. This is a totally new relationship, not picking up old threads.' Her heart was beating fast, her voice a little breathless, hoping that her mother wouldn't resist this change in her circumstances.

Rachel didn't speak while she lifted the turkey on to its carving board. A delicious savoury aroma engulfed them. Then she turned and gazed into her daughter's face earnestly. 'I accept that, and I just hope that you're right. I don't want you to live through that heartbreak that you experienced all those years ago.' She reached out and touched Elsa's cheek. 'You're still my little girl, even though you're taller than me, and I only want you to be happy.'

'Thanks, Mum.' Elsa threw her arms round her mother and they hugged tightly.

It was late afternoon when Graham arrived. After the introductions, he declared that although he'd enjoyed playing with his three-year-old grandson, the little boy had become fractious and tired so Graham was glad of some adult company to recover. But he said it with a fond smile, so they could tell that he thought the world of his family.

'Talking of grandchildren, have you two set a date for your wedding yet? I can't wait to get my outfit.' Rachel was handing round a box of Belgian chocolates.

'Mum, that's jumping the gun a bit. You're embarrassing Louise.' Jamie helped himself to two chocolates, not looking the least bothered by her remarks himself.

'Not at all. You know we want kids once we're married.' Louise was unfazed by her future mother-in-law's remarks. 'We've started looking at venues, and are thinking about a year in the spring, March or April. I love spring flowers, and this coming year would be too soon.'

They all laughed a lot that afternoon, and Elsa found herself watching Graham carefully in case he showed too much embarrassing affection to their mum in their presence. After the meal, he topped up Elsa's wine, waving away her protests. 'No need to worry; I'll run you home. I've been very good today, only one glass with lunch, so it's safe for me to drive. That means that Jamie and Louise can go straight home later.'

Elsa looked across at her mother, unable to erase the image that her mother could well be enjoying a new love life. Would they have liked to spend tonight together? But Rachel was quite relaxed, and at nine o'clock waved off Elsa and Graham happily. She only pecked his cheek, to Elsa's relief.

Elsa didn't say much on the way home, unable to totally relax with this man who could be her mother's lover. But as they approached Heronsburn, Graham cleared his throat and said, 'I know it must seem strange for you to see me with your mother, Elsa. But I want you to realise that I think a lot of her. She's an amazing person, and I enjoy her company very much.'

Startled, Elsa turned to look at him. 'It does seem a bit weird to me, Graham. But you're both mature people, and Mum had a really hard time with my dad after his accident. I couldn't expect her to stay on her own, and I suppose I could get used to her being in a relationship with someone else.' She hoped that her words were tactful, and hid the discomfort that she was feeling.

His expression brightened. 'Good. Because I'm hoping to stay around for quite some time. Now, is this the way to the seafront?'

Elsa kept the café closed for a

couple more days, and in that time she and Daniel managed a walk on the beach. They also went to one of the public skating sessions with Poppy and Ryan, his niece and nephew. Elsa couldn't believe how much she enjoyed herself, especially appreciating how good Daniel was with the children. He managed to create a fun experience for them without letting their antics on the ice get out of hand. The rink wasn't too packed, as most families were busy at home.

'What about New Year?' he asked her when he dropped her off at home. It was proving to be a busy festive season.

'That's Natalie's traditional party, and it's going to be a special one as Zach is going off to Australia on the second of January.'

'Will Zach mind if I'm there?'

'Of course not.' But despite her protestations, she couldn't help wondering that herself.

In the end, Zach was in an especially buoyant mood, telling them all about his holiday plans. He seemed perfectly relaxed talking with Daniel, even producing a rather wizened piece of mistletoe for a quick kiss from Elsa. Natalie and Mark's little semi-detached house was bursting with people from her work and some of his fellow teachers, as well as one or two neighbours and two of the skating group with their partners.

Once midnight had come and they popped champagne and streamers, the party settled into some serious dancing. At one o'clock, Daniel whispered in her ear, 'How do you feel about leaving now? I'd like to spend some time alone together.'

Elsa lifted her head from Daniel's shoulder, as they were dancing to a slow, dreamy number. Blinking contentedly at him, she replied, 'Sure. I need to give Missy her New Year treats.'

They made their farewells, grabbed their coats, and ran down the garden path, shivering in the crisp night air. The sharp cold shock roused her, and she found all her senses tingling with anticipation. It didn't take long to drive round to her flat, and they hurried inside. Missy was already tucked up in her basket, but she stood up, yawning, and came to meet them, weaving round Elsa's legs until she had given her the promised treats.

Daniel lounged on one arm against the kitchen counter, smiling lazily. Elsa looked up and their eyes met, sending a tingle down her spine.

'Now Missy's had her New Year gift, it's time for yours,' he said, pulling her into his arms and touching her lips with a feather-like kiss. 'Now, close your eyes.' She obliged, and heard a small 'snap' sound and a rustling before he continued. 'I didn't have time to get you anything special for Christmas, so I spent time in the past few days looking for the right gift.'

Elsa let herself be led over to the wall, where Daniel turned her round so that he was behind her. Then she felt a delicate touch on her neck.

'Okay, you can open your eyes now.'

Elsa did so and found herself looking at her reflection in her wall mirror. Her hand flew up to touch the delicate gold chain that was now suspended round her neck. Dangling from this was the most exquisite gold acorn, about the size of a coffee bean. 'Daniel, that's absolutely gorgeous! Thank you!' She swung round and pulled him towards her, kissing him delightedly.

He fingered the little pendant gently. 'I thought it had special significance for us — an acorn for new beginnings, a new year, and let's see what will grow.'

Then her face clouded. 'But I didn't get you anything special.'

'I really liked the shirt you bought me for Christmas — it's an unusual pattern. I need to liven up my wardrobe.'

'Well maybe you're just being polite. I don't know you well enough yet to know if you really mean that.' She searched his face for the answer to her conundrum.

He grinned, and leaned forward to nibble her ear playfully. 'Well, from now on we can begin to get to know each other as adults, instead of teenagers. I must say, I like what I've seen of you so far, Elsa.' He stifled any reply she would have given by pressing his lips to hers, and from there began a tender session of kissing and caressing.

About an hour later, they were cuddled up close on the settee, Elsa's head resting on Daniel's chest. Daniel cracked open an eye and groaned. 'I'm going to have to get going. Andrew and Vicki are bringing over the kids to my flat in the morning, and we're all going to see my aunt and uncle before meeting up with my parents for lunch.'

Elsa roused herself and accompanied him to the door of her flat, wrapping his scarf round his neck and pulling him towards her again. Her lips felt almost bruised with the amount of kissing they'd had that night, but it was a satisfying feeling.

'I have to go back to work on the

second of January,' he lamented. Carl Fitzsimmons had been in charge at the ice rink over New Year, giving Daniel some time off. 'But I promise I'll phone you this evening. When are you going skating again?' He was still holding her hand as they descended the steps to the front door.

'I have my usual supermarket delivery on the second, and the café will be opening again, so it means fresh baking. I'll probably go to the rink on Thursday evening. When is it closing?'

Daniel and Carl were introducing a new swipe card system, and they would need to close the rink for installation. 'Only on Tuesday and Wednesday next week, when the kids are back at school. It shouldn't disrupt business too much. The box office staff will need extra supervision during the first week or two, so Carl and I will be on call a lot. I'm afraid we won't be able to meet up as freely over the next few weeks.'

'I also have the café to think about — it would be so much easier if we both worked nine to five, Monday to Friday.' She felt reluctant to let him go, but disengaged her hand from his with an effort. The contact felt so right.

'Maybe it would be — but at least we're our own bosses.' They kissed lingeringly one final time, until he tore himself away from her and opened the door. 'We'll speak soon,' he promised as he walked to his car, now covered in frost.

Elsa woke up each day filled with joy as she looked forward to Daniel's phone calls and messages. He took her out for a drink after her skating practice. She longed to throw herself into this relationship, as it could be so fulfilling to be a couple as adults. But with their history and her uncertainty about what was going on at the ice rink, she knew that she had to hold something back.

That weekend it was the annual Heronsburn charity dip. Scores of brave souls would don fancy dress and hurl themselves into the bitter North Sea to raise money for local charities. It meant a busy day in the café, even though there were hot drinks laid on from mobile servers on the promenade. Luckily Katy was free to work, so each of them was able to take a turn to cheer on the swimmers before lunch.

It was a dry day with little wind, though there were some clouds to the west which looked as if they held rain. Elsa spotted the customary fire engine near the steps to the beach, surrounded by crowds of people. There were shrieks and cheers as the firemen turned on the hose to douse the swimmers before they took the plunge. Luckily the tide was in, so there wasn't too far to run to plunge into the sea. Already a stream of clowns, fairies, dogs and bears and various other characters were legging it towards the water.

Elsa noticed a familiar figure leaping up and down, cheering.

'Hi, Natalie — what's Mark's costume?'

Natalie turned to her, grinning. Her

nose was as pink as her woolly hat with the cold. 'Look, there he is — he's dressed as a cowboy this year.'

Looking down at the beach, she could see a figure with checked shirt, chaps and cowboy hat disappearing towards the waves. She joined her voice with her friend's. 'Come on, Mark!'

They watched him dive into the water, do a few strokes, then stagger back to his feet and make the wet and squelchy journey back towards the promenade. Delighted that she'd timed it perfectly, Elsa cheered him on, avoiding his cheeky attempt to hug her when he reached the top of the steps. Natalie wasn't so lucky, and shrieked as he threw a wet arm round her. Then she enveloped him in a large towel, and they headed off to the changing tent while Elsa turned to make her way back to the café. Lisa had already been down, but Katy was still waiting for her turn.

As she crossed the road in front of the café, a teenage girl with long fair hair approached her. She was wearing black leggings, a bright green fleece top, and was carrying a purple skating bag.

'You're in charge of the rainbow café, aren't you?' The girl's voice was a little hesitant.

'Yes, that's right.' Elsa smiled at her.

'I . . . I was wondering if there was the chance of a job at the weekends. I'm moving up to the Thursday night class next week, and I'd like to earn some money to pay for my skating.'

Surprised, Elsa asked the girl her name, and how old she was.

'Sky Ellis. I'm fifteen. I had my birthday last October.'

'And are your parents happy for you to take on a job?'

'Mam thought it would be a good idea when I told her over Christmas. I don't see much of my dad, and he's got a new family, so we don't have a lot of money. It was Mam who suggested asking you, as she's been in the café.'

They were nearing the door now. 'To be honest, Sky, I already have a student who works weekends. But I'll give it some thought. Give me your contact number.' She reached into her pocket for her phone, and tapped in the girl's home number.

Katy had told Elsa a few weeks earlier that she now had two free days a week at university, and had wondered if she could do some weekday work and have Sunday off, so possibly having another member of staff would work out. Elsa studied her accounts, and after a telephone call with her accountant, decided that it would be beneficial for the business to offer Sky a few hours each week.

Sky and her mother came round the following week for a formal interview. Elsa was impressed with the girl's manner, especially as both Sky and her mother vowed that she would take the job seriously. After Elsa had discussed her duties and pay, it was agreed that she would do a four-week trial, working three hours each Saturday and Sunday. There would be opportunities for extra work during the school holidays, especially to cover for any staff leave.

'I'm quite hopeful about her,' Elsa told Daniel when they next met. 'She began her training today, and seems bright enough, grasping how to work the till with no bother, and she took in all the hygiene regulations. We have some more training to do next Saturday, then she can start serving at tables.'

'Does this mean that you'll have more time off?'

She laughed. 'At the moment it's giving me more work, having another employee!' Then she became serious. 'Probably no more time off during café hours, but it should be less hectic for me when she settles in. Lisa will be able to help with the baking, and maybe I can be doing some paperwork at quiet times, so I could be freer in the evenings.'

'Good — and once the systems we're putting into place are running smoothly, maybe I'll be able to have more time off, too. I never sat down all weekend.' He yawned. 'With luck everything will settle down, and we'll be able to spend more time together.'

He looked deep into her eyes, and she felt herself melting, lost in him. How she longed to relax fully with him. Could she really abandon the niggling doubts that assailed her?

# 16

Whenever Elsa thought about the strange happenings at the ice rink, she worried about Daniel being alone there. When the late night hockey practices were on, he was often on his own upstairs in the office area. Carl's hours weren't regular as he had other businesses to take care of. Byron Newminster didn't have an office at the ice rink, as he had a more minor role in the consortium. The building was large and dark, with cold nooks and crannies where all sorts of mischief could take place. She really didn't believe Daniel had been involved in Arnie's death — but could someone else do the same to him?

However, as the weeks went by and there were no further sinister incidents at the ice rink, she began to relax. Most of her waking thoughts were of Daniel and their blossoming romance, and he even infiltrated her dreams. They texted each other several times a day, spoke at least once on the phone, and when they couldn't meet in person for several days, he posted little gifts through her letter box late at night — a little box of Belgian chocolates; a pair of brightly coloured ankle socks; a pretty clip for her hair; and even a catnip toy for Missy.

Daniel arranged to be free for Valentine's Day, and booked them into an upmarket restaurant in the city centre. She was waiting for him to arrive when she received a call from her mother.

'Elsa, I'm glad I caught you.' Rachel was aware that Elsa had a date.

She frowned. 'Is something wrong, Mum?' Her mother's voice sounded a little strange.

'No, not wrong. But I wanted to discuss something with you. I've been spending the day with Graham, and — well, he's asked me something.'

Blind panic brought a wave of dizziness to Elsa, and she sat down. It was Valentine's Day — Graham must have asked Rachel to marry him!

The thought overwhelmed her, and for a moment she couldn't take in what her mother was saying. Then she shook herself and began to listen to what Rachel was telling her.

'Of course, I thanked him very much, and said I'd run it past you and Jamie first. It was very nice of him, wasn't it?'

Heart pounding, Elsa managed to say, 'Mum, I didn't quite catch that. What did Graham ask you?'

'He asked me to accompany him when he goes to New Zealand next month to visit his cousin. Paul and his wife live in Christchurch. I've looked at the cost of the air fare, and I can afford it. Plus we would be staying with Paul and Eve, so I wouldn't have to fork out for hotels. What do you think?'

Elsa took a deep breath, thinking on her feet. So he wasn't asking Mum to marry him. Relief swamped her. 'It sounds like a lovely idea. How long would you be away for?'

'A whole month! I can't believe that I could actually be going to New Zealand. I've seen programmes on television, and it looks wonderful.'

'Just so long as you don't decide to stay there.' She tried to make her voice light, though it shook slightly. How serious was this relationship becoming?

'Then you don't mind? That's wonderful, I'll ring Jamie now and if he feels the same, I'll tell Graham that I'll go.'

Suddenly ashamed at her worries, Elsa added, 'Mum, you don't need to ask us. If you want to do it, you must. You deserve to enjoy yourself.' Both before and after her husband's death, Rachel had had a difficult and lonely time.

Her mother's voice was soft with gratitude as she replied. 'Thank you, darling. I appreciate that it must be strange for you to see me with another man.'

'Just go and enjoy yourself. I'm sure Jamie will say the same thing.' She was aware that she had avoided contradicting her mother, but her emotions were all over the place at present. She said goodbye and disconnected the call.

Elsa was still convincing herself that she really meant her words when Daniel arrived at the door with ten red roses. Suddenly all thoughts of her mother and Graham fled from her mind.

'Daniel, no one's ever bought me flowers on Valentine's Day before!'

He grinned at her delight. 'I know it's a cliché, and they're terribly overpriced, but I felt you deserved them for putting up with all my crazy hours and the number of times I've had to cancel our dates. But nothing's going to spoil tonight!'

Elsa felt delightfully pampered that evening at the restaurant, the meal perfectly cooked and the wine crisp and cool on her tongue. Looking into his eyes as they talked, the thought occurred to her that she had never felt so happy. At the moment she didn't even think about the future. It would have been tempting fate. Now was so wonderful, she wanted to live every moment to the full. Thoughts of her mother and Graham were pushed to the back of her mind.

The next day, they agreed to book tickets to go to a concert the following month of a group that they both liked. Every day their relationship was building more bonds, and Elsa felt that Daniel was planning that they would be together for some time.

'Be careful,' her mother said that evening when she rang to say that she had booked her holiday. 'Look what happened last time you were involved with Daniel.'

'He's changed — we both have. We were just kids then.'

'That may be so, but I worry about you being hurt again, Elsa. You've never really stopped wanting him, have you? All those other men you dated didn't compare with the image of Daniel that you always had.'

'I know what I'm doing, and I'm keeping a bit of myself back. I won't let myself fall in love with him until I know that there's a future.'

But as she replaced the phone, she realised that it was already too late. In the past few weeks she had been falling deeper and deeper into sheer, utter, devoted love for this man who was so attractive and kind. He now had depths that she found so compelling. But could she really let herself love him unreservedly? Was he ready to build a future with someone, or was he still carrying baggage from his divorce? Taking a deep breath, she told herself to stop thinking and just enjoy herself with Daniel.

At the end of the month she received a call from Zach, his first since returning from his holiday.

'So you enjoyed Australia?'

'Excellent! Back with a tan, a few extra muscles, and full of sea water from my attempts at surfing. Plus the telephone number of a bit of gorgeous totty from Manchester who I met on the plane coming home.'

'Zach! How rude!' But she was delighted that he was so upbeat. 'So are you going to ring her?'

'Already did — we're meeting up in York next Saturday. Yeah, you're right, I shouldn't call her 'totty', but she really is gorgeous. Tall, dark-haired, and she's called Amanda.'

'So will you be coming back to ice skating?'

'I'll see — it looks at the moment as if my weekends and my money may be required for other things.'

'I'm pleased for you, Zach. I hope it works out.'

'I hear you're involved with dishy Dan.'

She smiled at the term. 'We've been together since just before Christmas, and it seems to be going well.' The usual flutter of excitement caught her as she pictured him.

'Well, tell him if he breaks your heart again, he'll have me to deal with.'

'As long as you're not away meeting Amanda.'

'Well, that's true.' He chuckled.

It looked as if Zach was happy, which set her mind at rest, as she had worried that she had been unkind in keeping him dangling before Daniel and she got back together. She grabbed her skates and made for the ice rink, where she had an individual lesson booked with Laura. As she was sitting on one of the benches at the skate hire area to fasten her skates, she noticed that a piece of wood some twenty centimetres long was hanging off the bottom of one of the wooden bench blocks. She was bending down to get a better look, when someone came up beside her and thumped a toolbox down on the floor.

'I shouldn't touch that — you might hurt yourself,' came the gruff voice of Pete.

Elsa pulled her hand away quickly. 'Someone's been rough with it.'

He knelt down and took out his hammer and nails. 'Oh, they get kicked about a bit at the ice hockey games.' He fiddled with the piece of wood, trying to get it back in place.

'I think you might need to insert a new bit.'

He tussled with it for about a minute. 'Maybe you're right,' he said, sitting back on his haunches. At that moment, the door behind him opened and a young lad of about seventeen or eighteen appeared.

'I've been sent to help you, Grand-dad.' He looked surprised to see Elsa sitting putting on her skates. But that was nothing to the shock Elsa got when she looked at his face.

'Oh my goodness, what happened to you?'

His eye was bruised, going into colours of black, red and yellow, as it was obviously healing. He hung his head, seemingly unwilling to reply. His grandfather spoke up instead. 'I warned him to keep his nose clean — but our daughter told us he came home a few days ago with his face bashed in, and his only excuse was that he got into a fight at the pub.' The elderly man shook his head, and wagged a finger at his grandson. 'You're earning your own money, so we can't keep you on a leash, but you've got to realise that if you keep thc wrong company, you'll come a cropper. I hope this teaches you a lesson. And remember how this has upset your grandma.'

'Yes, Granddad,' was the muttered reply, clearly embarrassed at being the centre of attention.

'Anyway, as you're here, you can get me a piece of wood to mend this bench. There are some scrap pieces just inside the door of my room. Bring me two or three bits so we can decide which to use.' He began rummaging in his toolkit and took out a hammer. Then he noticed that Elsa was ready, so he gave her a pointed look. 'We'll be making a bit of a mess, so you'd better take your stuff into the ice rink.'

Realising that he wanted rid of her, Elsa stood up. 'I was going anyway, as I'm having a lesson now.' She began to walk to the door to the ice, then suddenly had a thought and turned back to him. 'Pete, you're here a lot when the public aren't around. Have you noticed any odd people here who maybe aren't working on the renovations?'

He looked away. 'We've had a lot of new people coming in — decorators, engineers and such. It's hard to keep track of them all.'

'You don't think there's something going on that shouldn't be, do you?'

He frowned, then stood up. 'No, nothing.' His voice was terse, and she didn't know whether it was because he was angry at her questioning him, or because he knew something and was hiding it from her. But he clearly wasn't going to give her any information, so she let it go and turned to walk through to the ice.

# 17

Daniel started visiting other ice rinks round the country to see if there were any useful ideas, which meant a few days away each time. 'Of course, lots of them are part of a leisure centre, so they get funding from the local authority and make money from other activities that go on. While some family members are skating, others can be swimming or using a climbing wall, or attending a fitness class.'

'Well, you can't have a swimming pool, but surely some of the rooms could be used for other activities like yoga or Zumba,' Elsa suggested.

'Yes, the upstairs rooms have now been renovated, and we're planning some trial courses in the summer. Carl is putting together some ideas, and his wife has some contacts for instructors. We've started some off-ice fitness classes for the youngsters. Tom and Alex, our coaches, have been wanting to introduce that for a while, and Irina was all for it. The usual summer training camps for ice hockey and figure skating are booked into the schedule. There will also be some day courses for the more elementary skaters, including adults, during the summer.'

His face lit with excitement as he talked, and he was even proposing that they could build a climbing wall out at the back the following year, if all went well financially. 'It would bring in a whole new clientele. Of course, we'd need to upgrade the other customer services like the toilets and the cafeteria, plus expanding the shop further to include the new sports.' Monica had now retired and a man in his fifties had taken over.

The ice rink was looking much more modern than it had done before Daniel's consortium took over. Now that it was running more smoothly, Daniel insisted on taking Elsa away for a few days to the Lake District. 'You deserve a proper break,' he argued. 'I bet you haven't had a holiday since you started the café.'

It was true. Lisa was perfectly capable, and there was plenty of baking in the freezer. They stayed from Sunday to Wednesday so she only had to miss one full opening day of the café. Her assistant was also happy to feed Missy, make a fuss of the little cat, and let her out a couple of times each day. She would text regularly to let Elsa know that all was well.

They left after lunch on the Sunday. It only took a couple of hours to drive to Cumbria, so it was still light when they arrived. Elsa gasped in delight when she saw the soaring mountains, dwarfing the traditional small hotel near Lake Windermere. The water of the lake was ruffled by a brisk wind, but reflected deep blue to match the sky. As she gazed from the window of the hotel dining room, the mood of the lake was changing by the minute as clouds raced by overhead.

Next morning they took the ferry across the lake and walked up a mountain path. The route was popular, thronged with other walkers, couples of all ages, dog walkers, and a few larger groups of ramblers.

Elsa was glad she'd packed a pair of walking boots at Daniel's instruction. 'They're just the waterproof boots I use when I walk on the beach,' she warned. 'I hope they'll be up to it.'

'We're not going to do anything too tough — there are plenty of walkers' paths.'

When they reached the highest point, her breath was taken away not just with the exertion, but also with the vastness of the view. Some clouds had begun to streak across the blueness of the sky, but rays of sun were breaking through the cloud and sparkling on the lake beneath them. Mountains soared up from the lakeside, pulling the eye upwards. They stopped to regain their breath, and Daniel put an arm round her, holding her tightly.

'That last bit was tough. How are you doing?'

She gave a wry smile. 'I'm not used to climbing. I'll feel it tomorrow.'

He returned her smile and touched her lips lightly with his own. 'Let's stop for lunch now. There's a good spot.' He removed his rucksack and reached in for their waterproofs, which Elsa arranged on the ground. Once they had sat down, he passed her the ham rolls they had bought before they took the ferry.

They sat in silence while they ate, sharing a bottle of water and savouring the vista before them. The sounds around them were muted in the open air. Occasionally other walkers would say hello on their way past.

Elsa gave a sigh of contentment. 'This was a wonderful idea, Daniel — just what I need. Thank you.'

'Me too. But I can see that there's something worrying you. What's up?'

She bit her lip. There were so many

problems churning around in her mind. But she realised that there was one thing she really wanted to share with him. 'It's my mum. You know she and Graham have been seeing each other for some time? She's going on holiday to New Zealand with him soon to visit his cousin. It's for a whole month!'

He looked at her with a quizzical expression. 'So what's worrying you — that they're going for a month, or that she's going with him at all?'

Elsa wrapped her arms around herself, looking away. 'Lots of things, really. First, that I think that they stay at each other's houses sometimes, so obviously they must be sleeping together. Then, they must be serious about each other if they're going to visit family on the other side of the world. And lastly, why am I being so horrid about it when I know my mum deserves happiness just like anyone else?'

'Whew! That's a lot!' He reached out one arm and drew her close, so that she was cradled in his arms, resting his chin on the top of her head. 'I can understand all your emotions. I know how close you were to your dad. Everything you did or achieved, you wanted to share it with him. He was a fighter, and never let his disability hold him back. I remember him cheering you on at the school sports days, and coming to the school fairs. He was so proud when you won that cake competition when you were fifteen!'

Elsa's eyes blurred with tears as she smiled at this recollection. 'Fancy you remembering that! We weren't dating then.'

'No, but I had my eyes on you for some time. You were all legs and carroty curls, but I fancied you like mad.'

She gave a gulp of laughter, wiping the moisture from her eyes.

'But I can imagine how hard it must have been for your mum. Your dad couldn't go back to his job as a sales rep, and his arms weren't that strong either, after the accident. He was ill a lot, wasn't he?'

'Yes, he had lots of infections. I realise now that Mum had so much on her plate, looking after him, working full time, and she had two teenagers to worry about as well, though we did our best to help.'

'No wonder she finds it hard to forgive me for hurting you — I must have added a lot to her burden by leaving you in the lurch.'

'Oh, Daniel, that's just part of growing up. It's all in the past now.'

He hugged her tighter. 'I can understand why you feel ambiguous about Graham. It must be hard to see your mum moving on. I'm sure he's not trying to take your father's place — he's got his own family. He obviously cares a lot about your mum, and wants to make her happy.'

'But do you think that Mum's putting Dad behind her?'

'I'm positive she's not. She and your dad made a life and a family, so he'll always be a part of her life. This is just a new chapter for her. Do you remember my Aunt Sheila, who lives in Southampton? Her husband died of a brain tumour when my cousins were in their teens. But she met and married a great guy ten years later, and it's all worked out really well. Don't you think it would be nice if your mum and Graham could have a happy future together instead of being lonely and bitter?'

After a moment, Elsa replied, 'Yes, I see that now. Of course Mum won't forget Dad, just like Jamie and I won't.' Impulsively she hugged him back. 'Thanks for helping me to talk it through. I feel much better about it now.' Their holiday together had been wonderful, but his unexpected under-standing of her worries had forged deeper bonds between them.

On their final morning, Daniel's mobile rang while they were packing the car. Listening to the caller, his face became solemn, his voice terse as he made monosyllabic replies to the person on the other end.

He disconnected the call. 'That was Carl. There's been a power failure in the plant. There's an ice hockey match on Friday night, and the team are anxious to train. I'm sorry, but we won't be able to call in at Louise and Jamie's — I'll need to get to the ice rink as soon as possible.'

'Of course.' Elsa swallowed her disappointment. She'd been looking forward to sharing him with her brother and his fiancée.

Daniel was preoccupied for most of the journey, which made Elsa suspect that there was something he hadn't mentioned to her. It wasn't until he phoned her the next morning that she discovered what was going on.

'Were you planning on skating this morning?'

'Yes; I have a private lesson next week and want to do some practice.'

'The ice won't be ready until tomorrow. Someone sabotaged the plant, and we've had to pull strings to get the machinery repaired at short notice.'

'*Sabotaged?* How could that happen?'

His voice was grim. 'Luckily it wasn't so serious that it was past repair, but some important parts needed to be replaced. The ice is forming again now, but it's not ready for skating yet. This was an expense we could have done without.'

Elsa had to content herself with waiting until the next day. There was plenty of baking to do, so she knuckled down to that. But as she measured her ingredients, chopping, mixing, pouring, her mind was on the troubles at the rink. Couldn't Daniel see that something needed to be done? Someone could be badly hurt, or the rink could lose a lot of money. She suppressed the idea that Daniel could be involved in something shady, and this was why he didn't want to have more security or police on the premises. After all, he had seemed shocked by what had occurred, and she didn't believe he would deceive her.

Daniel took her to the ice hockey match on the Friday night, but she sensed that he wasn't really with her in thought. He left her standing in the foyer for a long time at the end. She was beginning to wish that she had just walked home on her own, when she heard the sound of raised voices beyond the doors, near the rink entrance. Worried that Daniel was involved, she opened the swing door as softly as she could and looked tentatively down the corridor. Immediately she realised that neither of the voices was Daniel's. The two men were Carl and Robert Fitzsimmons. Identical in height, their eyes were locked, so they were oblivious of her presence.

'I've had enough of your stalling! Do you want this place to fail?' Carl, heavier in build, grabbed the two sides of his brother's denim jacket. Whippet thin, Robert tore himself away from Carl's grip and pointed a bony finger at him. His face was contorted with hatred.

'Keep your hands off me! You're a traitor to this family. All that's happened is your fault, bringing in strangers and breaking our mother's heart. I regret that you ever persuaded me to sign so much over to them. You'll ruin us!' So saying, he turned on his heel and headed towards the exit.

In the split second that he began to move, Elsa jerked back out of sight, so that she was standing just outside the door. She looked towards him as he emerged, but he merely glared at her and stalked towards the main door, shoving it open and letting it swing shut with a bang behind him.

Breathless, she turned round again at the sound of the door behind her, and was astonished to find Daniel emerging. He smiled at her. 'Sorry about that — just a bit of business to take care of. I hope you weren't too bored waiting.'

'I was nearly knocked off my feet by Robert Fitzsimmons. Did you hear him rowing with Carl just now in the corridor?' They emerged into the cold night air. It was just beginning to rain, so she pulled up her hood to cover her hair.

Daniel paused to lock the door. 'I did see Carl, but I must have just missed their altercation. I was speaking with one of the maintenance staff. Robert was probably in a foul mood because the team lost. They've had a poor run over the past six games, and it reflects badly on him.'

Elsa thought that Daniel's expression was taut, despite his attempt at lightness. She decided not to tell him about Robert's antagonism towards the consortium. He was astute enough to know about that anyway, she guessed. They began the walk to her flat, his arm around her shoulder.

'You would tell me if there was anything troubling you, wouldn't you?' she asked.

He squeezed her arm. 'You don't need to worry about me, Elsa. I'm fine.

It's tough in the first year of business, as you well know.'

'That's true,' she murmured, and they walked the rest of the way in companionable silence. They indulged in a long kiss at the door before he went to his car, which he had left in the side street to make more room in the rink car park.

Next day she let herself daydream with thoughts of Daniel as she did her Saturday morning baking, surrounded by delicious aromas of cinnamon and pastry. Katy and Lisa were on duty in the café, and Sky came in at lunchtime. The girl seemed to be enjoying her job, and began to chat to Elsa about the ice rink when they were in the kitchen together.

'Bethany's been talking about moving down to London,' Sky told her. 'To be honest, I'd be glad if she went. At first I thought that she was really cool, and a group of us used to hang out with her, and sometimes watch her train. But I didn't like what she did to Tara.'

Astonished, Elsa paused in emptying the dishwasher, pushing back a curl that had dampened from the steam, so that she could look at Sky. 'Do you mean that threatening note in Tara's bag at Christmas? Bethany wasn't anywhere near it — I was in the changing room with her.'

Sky was loading a tray with clean cups and saucers to take through to the counter. 'She asked me to slip the note into Tara's bag — I didn't know what was written on it, but I suspected it wasn't nice. I knew how she talked about her, so I said no. In the end, it was Morgan who did it. We were really freaked out when we heard what it had said, 'coz we like Tara, but Bethany threatened to deny any knowledge of it and say that it was our idea, if we told anyone.'

'Then I hope that she does move away.'

'I think she will. She says Herons-burn is a dead end, and I know she wants to get on the national team.'

# 18

'Remember I won't be here next week — Mark and I are off to Thailand on Thursday.'

Natalie and Elsa were walking home from their Sunday skating lesson.

'Is it that time already? I'd forgotten that you'd booked a holiday for April.' A salty breeze caught them as they turned the corner towards the café.

'Yes, I can't wait. I seem to have done nothing but work and skate recently, and I'm shattered. A couple of weeks lazing on the beach will be great.'

Natalie did look tired, Elsa thought, and her usual bounce was diminished. Since Elsa had revived her relationship with Daniel, the two women had seen less of each other. She hugged Natalie and wished her a good holiday, and within moments was swallowed up into her everyday life again at the café.

The following week, Elsa was getting ready to go out with Daniel whilst looking through the letters that the postman had delivered that morning. A white envelope with a handwritten address caught her eye. She didn't recognise the writing, and it certainly didn't look like a bill.

Quickly she slit it open, and could hardly believe what she was reading.

'*Northern County News*

Dear Elsa Turnfield,

'Each year the newspaper sponsors an evening of awards in conjunction with the north eastern branch of the British Tourist Association. We ask the public for nominations, and send out 'mystery shoppers' to sample the services, to go towards an award for the best small businesses in the area. We are delighted to inform you that the Rainbow Café, Heronsburn, has reached the final of the best café division this year.'

Elsa nearly dropped the letter in her surprise. It went on to give information about the date of the award, which would be at one of the city centre hotels. She could take a guest, and there was an email address to contact with her acceptance.

Daniel noticed that she had some important news when she climbed into his car. 'You're looking very smug,' he said, kissing her briefly on the lips.

She made him wait until they were sitting in their seats at the cinema before showing him the letter. 'I can hardly believe it! The winner will get a plaque, but even if I don't win I can put in my publicity that the café was a finalist in the competition.'

Daniel's responding grin delighted her. He leaned over and pulled her into his arms, regardless of the people around them. 'Well, you deserve it, as your café is one of the best I've ever seen. It doesn't matter that it's small, your cooking is fantastic, and it looks really attractive.'

He put the date in his calendar, then brought a folded piece of newspaper from his pocket. It was an article that had appeared in the local paper, under the byline of Nathan Troutbeck. 'This is the journalist who interviewed you, isn't it?'

'Yes, that's the one. I must admit, he did me a favour, as business picked up even more after his feature.' She looked at the headline. *New Brooms at the Ice Rink*. 'Did he interview you?'

'No. He asked me, but I was too busy, so he spoke to Carl a few days ago. I've read it, and he seems to have included all the innovations that we've introduced.'

'Oh, look, there's a picture of you and Carl. How did he get that?'

'There was a report in the paper when the consortium took over, and we were photographed at a meeting of the Chamber of Commerce.'

Elsa remembered how Nathan had tried to quiz her about Daniel, and his suspicions that something shady was going on at the ice rink. This article was quite open, so maybe he had shelved his investigations in that line. But the next day, when she was emerging after an evening practice session, she noticed a man sitting in a car by the gate to the parking area, and with a jolt recognised Nathan Troutbeck. He was talking on his phone and not looking towards her, so she hurried off before he might think of accosting her. Her pulse racing with anxiety, she walked back home as quickly as she could.

Elsa's mother left for her holiday in New Zealand with Graham at the beginning of April. 'I'll probably manage to email you a few times, and if I'm bold enough I might try using Skype when we're staying with Graham's cousin.'

'Great! I've always fancied using it. It would be a good way to keep in touch with Daniel too when he goes away on some of his trips, instead of just phoning and texting.'

Despite her upbeat words, Elsa felt rather bereft at the realisation that her mother would be on the other side of the world. But at least Natalie was due back from Thailand soon. She'd already sent her a text about the award nomination, and had received back an enthusiastic reply.

Natalie texted when she and Mark arrived home on the Thursday before Easter, confirming that they would meet at the usual place for Sunday skating class. But before Elsa left home, a message came up on her phone. *'Sorry, can't make it today — must have picked up a bug on holiday.'* Elsa sent back an expression of sympathy. *'Take care, see you soon, Elsa xx.'* Poor Natalie, she thought as she walked along the road. No wonder she had been so uncommunicative since arriving home. Usually she would have been on the phone, gushing about how great her holiday was. She was always so full of life.

By the following weekend, Elsa hadn't heard anything from Natalie, and was beginning to feel worried. She'd texted a few times, and had brief replies, but she really wanted to talk with her. On Saturday she found a moment to phone, and Mark answered.

'Oh, hi Mark. It's Elsa. How's Natalie? Is she over her bug yet?'

'I'll just get her.'

When Natalie came to the phone, she sounded distant, her voice quite unlike the person Elsa had grown so close to. 'I'm still feeling under the weather. It's really pulled me down. I've been off work all week, and I certainly won't be coming skating yet.'

'Oh, Natalie, that's such a shame. I do hope you'll be feeling better soon. Shall I come round tomorrow?'

'No, I'm not really up to seeing anyone at the moment. Mark's looking after me fine.'

After a few further words, Elsa rang off, her mood sinking. Lifting up Missy, who was rubbing round her ankles, she hugged the cat and spoke into her fur. 'Poor Natalie! It's not like her to be ill. I hope she gets over it soon.'

Daniel was busy for the next few

days, but Elsa was occupied with her accountant preparing her figures for the end of the year, and went for an evening session at the ice rink on the Tuesday. When she emerged after her practice, she noticed a dark blue car parked up at the top of the car park in the growing dusk. She was certain that this was the one that the journalist had been sitting in last time she had seen him. Then she noticed him disappearing behind the rink. Resentful of his suspicions of Daniel, she followed him, and found him trying one of the back doors.

'What are you doing?' she demanded. 'You're not very subtle about your investigations, you know!'

Nathan whirled round, his mouth set in a strict line. 'Shush! You could spoil everything!' His voice was a hoarse whisper.

But before she could reply, the door swung open and Carl Fitzsimmons appeared in the doorway. 'What's going on here? Who are you?' His brow was furrowed as he glared at Nathan Troutbeck. He didn't even glance at Elsa.

'I thought I saw an open door, and wanted to make sure everything was all right,' the journalist explained. Elsa marvelled at Nathan's cool. 'This young lady was helping me, as she knows the manager.'

Furious that he had involved her, Elsa was about to make an angry denial of any involvement, then realised that might sound worse.

'Well, there's nothing going on — and this door wasn't open at all. You're mistaken.'

Nathan gave a cheery smile, apologising for his mistake. Grabbing Elsa's arm, he walked away briskly. Within a few paces, she managed to shake him off. 'What do you mean by implicating me?' she hissed. 'It was nothing to do with me!'

'Better to make it as innocent as possible.' He spoke out of the side of his mouth.

When they had turned the corner, she rounded on him furiously. 'Don't ever treat me like that again! He's quite right, you have no justification for snooping round here.'

'Well, you can deny it all you like, but I know that there's something shady going on here. I'll prove you wrong.'

'You're just after a story!' She stalked off, fuming. How dare he poke around — he was trying to pin something on Daniel, which was unfair as he had worked hard to make the place a going concern. Head down, she almost bumped into Pete's grandson coming out of the newsagents' shop with a sandwich and a packet of crisps.

'Oh, hello Sean. How are you now?' The bruises had faded from his face.

Startled at her question, he stopped, staring at her for a few seconds as if bemused.

'I'm Elsa — your grandma works for me at the Rainbow café. I saw you with your granddad after you'd had the trouble at the pub — remember?'

'I'm all right,' he mumbled, looking down. A broad, squat man emerged behind him from the shop, also with a sandwich.

'Come on, Sean, no time to stand gossiping.' He put his free hand on Sean's shoulder, digging his fingers into the lad's sweatshirt and propelling him towards the ice rink.

Elsa sighed. She was only trying to be friendly, but didn't seem to be getting very far. Well, at least she would get a devoted welcome from her cat when she arrived back home.

Daniel was to attend a big convention in America, which he talked about excitedly. 'It's in Idaho, at the Sun Valley Ice Rink, an outdoor rink that's open all year round. The U.S. Figure Skating Society is meeting, and this year they're allowing some delegates from overseas. I contacted them to request a place as an observer, and explained my situation. Even though we're small fry here in Heronsburn, they were quite happy for me to go. I wish you could come with me, Elsa.'

Elsa had been open on the May bank holiday Monday, so she had decided to close the café on the Tuesday instead. Daniel had taken the afternoon off, and they were walking on the sands at Alnmouth, a pretty village further up the coast in Northumberland. Holding Daniel's hand, Elsa felt invigorated, sucking in great lungsful of fresh sea air. The sky was a deep vibrant blue, the brisk wind whipping tendrils of hair round her face. Stepping over a piece of seaweed, she tucked her scarf into her neck to keep out the chill in the breeze.

'It sounds wonderful — but I can't get away for any length of time at the moment. The café is doing well, and having a weekend assistant has been a good move. But we're not big enough for another full-time staff member.'

'You certainly have the successful touch. I liked your idea of some home-baked cakes for the ice rink cafeteria, too. I've been doing some pricing . . . '

'Oh, let's forget about work for a while. Come on, I'll race you down to the water!' The tide was far out, and before he could reply, she pulled away and began running towards the sea, laughing. The wind caught her hat, leaving her auburn curls streaming out behind her.

Daniel paused to pick up her hat, and came up behind her as she danced at the edge of the waves. 'Unfair!' he laughed. 'That was a ploy to make me slow down.' He grabbed her and pulled her into his arms, tasting her cold lips with his own. Her mouth was warm, salty from the sea air, and he slid his tongue inside before pulling back suddenly as a larger wave threatened to run over their boots. 'The tide's coming in.'

Putting his arm round her shoulders, he held her close as they walked back to the car. Afterwards, he took her back to his flat where he cooked them a meal.

Wiping her lips, replete and happy, Elsa remarked, 'That was delicious. You have hidden depths, Daniel. Any more talents I have still to discover?'

He grinned wolfishly, taking her plate. 'Plenty more yet. Just you wait!'

Understanding what he implied, her cheeks glowed. He placed a chocolate mousse in front of her, and another on his own place mat.

'I confess that I bought these at the supermarket — their best range, though!'

They laughed, but once he had poured them both a coffee and slid back into his seat opposite her, his mood became serious.

'Elsa, you know that you suspected there was something odd going on at the ice rink?'

She nodded, her heart beginning to race with anxiety. 'You've discovered what it is?'

He shook his head. 'No, despite all my investigations. But I'm not convinced, and it would be a good idea if you kept to the main public areas and didn't come behind the scenes anymore. The corridors can be dark and lonely at times, and I wouldn't want you to be involved in another incident like that one at Halloween.'

Elsa shifted indignantly in her seat. 'Daniel, I'm not the one who's working there all the time! You're making me scared, thinking of you alone in your office at all sorts of odd hours.'

He placed his hands on her shoulders, looking deep into her eyes. 'I promise that I'm being careful — I won't pull any late nighters any more if Carl isn't there, or else I'll go when the ice hockey practices are on and work in the room that the box office staff use. But you're far more vulnerable, and I'd never forgive myself if anything happened to you.'

She hugged him close. 'All right — but I want you to text me if you're going to be there late, and let me know when you're safe at home. I wish you would call in the police.'

He gave a long sigh. 'I would if I could find any evidence. I suppose if nothing else happens after a certain length of time, we can assume that it was just a few freak incidents because we were letting in strangers to do the renovations.'

When he took her back home, she held him more tightly, and tried to hide her concerns when he said goodbye.

The date of the award dinner arrived, and Elsa closed the café half an hour earlier so she had plenty of time to get ready. She was wearing her one decent occasion dress, a short black number with wrist-length lace sleeves. Reluctantly she had taken off the gold acorn necklet that Daniel had given her at New Year, and that she had worn every day since. She had chosen to wear her pearl earrings with a matching pearl and gold pendant on a fine chain, plus new black sheer tights and her patent heels. The outfit didn't have the 'zing' of the green silk dress she'd borrowed from Natalie for the Chamber of

Commerce Christmas dinner dance, but it had felt like intruding to think about contacting her friend to ask to borrow it again. Thinking of Natalie brought to the fore the uneasy concern that roiled constantly at the back of her mind. Elsa noticed in the mirror that she was frowning, and turned away to rummage for her make-up bag. Anyway, the event was a six o'clock start, so not really for evening wear.

While applying the last stroke of mascara, her mobile buzzed and rang on the dressing table beside her. It was Daniel.

'Elsa, I'm so sorry — something really important has come up at work, and we need to call an emergency meeting.'

The pit of her stomach felt as if it was dropping down a great abyss. 'Oh, no, Daniel, not for this evening?'

'I know, it's your awards presentation, and I was really wanting to be there with you. I think it'll be over by eight. I'll come round to your place afterwards, and wait until you get back.'

Disappointment washed over her like a huge wave. She had been looking forward so much to sharing this with Daniel, and it seemed so empty to have to experience it all on her own. But he was adamant that he was needed for this meeting, so she agreed to see him later. It was a few minutes before she could rouse herself from the depths to apply her lipstick, but at last she did so and called a taxi.

The presentation was taking place in one of the new chrome and glass hotels beside the river, and the excitement of the occasion finally blew away the fog that engulfed her. The hotel lobby was vast, the glass front of the hotel displaying a magnificent view of the sunlit river as she climbed the stairs from the lobby to the first floor conference room. Here, more windows framed the silhouette of an imposing bridge beyond the hotel. Ten tables were laid with places, and a man in a suit with a clipboard directed her to her place. A pang caught her as she noticed the place beside her, labelled 'Guest', but she decided that she had mourned Daniel's absence long enough. She was determined to enjoy her evening.

To her delight, she discovered that one of the women she had met at the Chamber of Commerce Christmas dinner was also seated at her table. Her name was Tabitha, owner of a guest house just up the coast from Herons-burn, and they were soon chatting like old friends.

When it came to the awards them-selves, Elsa was astonished and delighted to receive a silver award as runner up in the café division. When her name was called, she didn't register it for a moment, until Tabitha nudged her with a delighted grin, and prompted, 'Go on, it's you! Well done!'

Blinking at the lights and the applause, Elsa squeezed round the seats of the other nominees and their guests, and climbed the steps to the platform slightly unsteadily. The flash of a camera made her blink as she accepted her plaque and a framed certificate from a local football star who was doing the presentations. He kissed her on both cheeks, and winked cheekily. Thank goodness she wasn't expected to make a speech! That was left for the winner of the top award, owner of a cyclists' café in County Durham.

Afterwards, Elsa accepted a lift back to Heronsburn from Tabitha, who had given her a business card and promised to be in touch in the next few weeks to meet up. As they passed the ice rink, Elsa noticed Daniel's car parked outside, so asked Tabitha to drop her there. She couldn't wait to show him her plaque and certificate! He'd be so thrilled for her.

It was now nearing nine o'clock, and the box office was about to close, but Jean smiled at her and said that Daniel was still upstairs. Elsa walked along past the rink, noticing that there were a few people leaving the ice. Then she took the stairs to the upper corridor, which was deserted. It was dark and cold, which made her remember Daniel's words about it being unsafe for her there, and felt a shiver up her spine. Although the corridor was unlit, there was light ahead of her, and she realised that the source was Daniel's office, where the door was ajar.

She approached the opening softly, and became aware of a woman's voice speaking, and Daniel's deep voice making quiet replies. Putting a finger to the door, not wishing to intrude, she pushed it slightly so that she could see what was going on — and drew in her breath sharply at the scene she beheld. Daniel was holding Irina close to him, stroking her hair and murmuring into her ear.

With a ragged gasp of dismay, she stepped backwards and ran back down the corridor before they could notice her. Heart pounding, she hurried through the now deserted corridors to the foyer, and fled outside. The door banged behind her, but she didn't stop until she reached home. Pulling off her high heels and discarding them, she threw herself on to her sofa, dragging in sobbing breaths as she tried to understand what she had seen. Had he been warning her off visiting him at the rink because he was involved with Irina again? How could Daniel betray her now, just when her heart had been given so completely? She would never, ever forgive him.

# 19

When she saw Daniel's number come up on her ringing mobile later that evening, she nearly ignored it, but in the end gave in because she had to know what was going on.

'Elsa, it's me. I'm really sorry, but I'm going to have to cancel tonight. I know it's our last evening before I fly to America, but something really important has come up.'

'Oh yes? And what's that?' Her voice was hard.

'I — well, I've got to take Irina — '

'Irina! I knew it!' She didn't give him time to finish. 'All this fake concern for me, I know it's just to keep me away from seeing what's going on with you and her. Don't try and explain!' She cut off his reply. 'I saw you earlier with her, all over her.'

'What — what do you mean?' He

sounded bewildered. *He's such a good actor*, she told herself.

Her voice was shaking with anger and hurt as she replied. 'I stopped off at the ice rink to tell you about the presentation that you missed because you said you had something more important to do. To share with you that I came second, and got a plaque for the café.'

'But that's wonderful. Elsa, I'm so proud of you.'

'Well, you've got a funny way of showing it. I saw you with Irina in your arms. I suppose you thought that you could scare me off and keep me away from the ice rink while you keep up your affair with her. Well, you're not going to play around with my feelings any more, Daniel. We're through. You can go off to America and take her with you, for all I care!' So saying, she disconnected the call, though her hand was shaking so much she could still hear his voice denying her accusations for a few seconds before she managed to tap the right button.

Her phone rang again immediately, but she switched it off. There was nothing he could say to get out of this — she had seen it with her own eyes. She was still sitting hunched over with her arms wrapped round herself, tears streaming down her face, when Missy jumped up beside her and rubbed her face on Elsa's elbow. She gathered the little animal into her arms and moaned, great wrenching sobs tearing from her as she tried to gain some comfort from the presence of her faithful pet.

Two days later, Daniel had left the country, and Elsa, alone in her flat, was missing him more than she had thought possible. A great aching hole had opened up in her life, and her future, instead of looking bright as it had done a few days ago, was a vast desert devoid of love and companionship. Many texts and voicemails had come through before he left, but she had steeled herself to delete them all without opening them. She told herself that she had been a fool to think that anyone could get back together with their first love and make a go of it.

*Silly romantic nonsense*, she muttered as she cracked eggs to make a sponge cake. White and dark chocolate, a new recipe, and to hang the fact that Daniel loved chocolate — he'd never taste it. The ice rink was forced to the back of her mind. At least she had her business to fill her thoughts, to block out the pictures of the beautiful outdoor ice rink at Sun Valley in Idaho. Whenever she was on the computer, her fingers itched to search for it, but she knew it would only make her feel worse if she saw the real thing.

The day after Daniel left, Elsa realised that it was more than a month since she had seen Natalie. Worry for her friend resurfaced, so as soon as she had finished for the day, she telephoned Natalie's home. Mark answered.

'It's Elsa, Mark. How's Natalie? I tried phoning three times last week, and left messages for her — did she get them?'

'Thanks for ringing, Elsa.' His voice was low and dispirited. 'She hasn't felt like talking to anyone. I've been worried about her, but she didn't want me to tell anyone.'

A pang of worry spiked in Elsa. 'Could I speak with her again?'

'No, she's not here — she's having a few days in hospital.'

'Oh, Mark, why didn't you let me know?' Elsa's voice was choked. 'What ward is she in?'

'Elsa, she really doesn't want to see anyone at the moment. I'm hoping that the treatment will help her. I'll tell her that you've been concerned and hopefully when she's home, she'll feel able to talk again.'

Elsa put down the phone and sat immobile, hugging her knees. This was worse than she could imagine! It sounded serious — especially as Natalie didn't want to talk with her, when they had been so close. She wondered if her friend was disappointed that Elsa had spurned Zach and turned to Daniel.

Surely not, as Zach was happy with Amanda. She tried phoning him, but there was no reply. She left a message to ring her as soon as possible. Maybe he could shed some light on the matter.

Elsa avoided the ice rink as the joy had gone out of skating without Natalie and Daniel. It only reminded her that one wouldn't speak to her, and the other had let her down. However, after returning from a trip into town two days later, she forgot to get off the bus a stop earlier and take a short cut. There was nothing else to do but get off at the rink. There were a few vehicles in the car park, probably for an ice hockey training session. Then she drew in her breath as she saw a familiar car. How could it be? Daniel's car was sitting in the car park, bold as brass, and he was supposed to be in America.

Sharply, she turned away and ran all the way back to the café. Had he been lying to her about going to America? The more she thought about it, the more clues seemed to point to Daniel being involved in the mysterious events at the ice rink — so maybe he had had a part in Arnie's death after all. She could have been dating a murderer all these months. Irina was welcome to him!

In Elsa's more rational moments, she just felt miserable. When her mother contacted her via Skype, Elsa had to confess that she and Daniel had stopped dating, and that their attempts to rekindle their former love had been disastrous. Thankfully her mother didn't say 'I told you so' and had just commiserated without making a drama of it. Elsa was wishing that they could talk it over, because somehow this breakup seemed to be a bigger deal. But instead she put on a brave face, and also said little about Natalie's illness as she didn't want to spoil her mother's holiday. Afterwards, she realised that she had never seen Rachel looking so happy, smiling and laughing, so relaxed with Graham. Whatever happened, this was right for her mother, and Elsa acknowledged that this was some comfort to her right now.

The next evening, she took some flowers for Natalie round to Mark, and was surprised when he invited her in. 'Natalie came out of hospital yesterday, but she's still rather fragile.'

When Elsa entered their sitting room, she found Natalie watching television, sitting with her feet up on the settee. Elsa sat down beside her and gave her a warm hug. 'I've been so worried about you. I brought you some flowers.'

Natalie's face had grown thinner, and the smile she gave was weak. 'That's nice. Thanks.'

Elsa rattled on for a while about the café, and mentioned that she wasn't going out with Daniel anymore. But nothing brought more than a few words from her friend. After about ten minutes, seeing the faraway look in Natalie's eyes, she realised with a sinking heart that she couldn't rouse a spark from her. 'Well, you're obviously tired, so I'll go. You will let me know if you want anything?'

Natalie appeared to lift her gaze with difficulty, and she only looked at her for a few seconds before lowering her lashes. 'Thanks. Thanks for coming round.' Her voice drifted away. With another hug, Elsa left the room and put her head round the kitchen door, where Mark was sitting with a pile of exercise books, doing some marking.

'I'm off now, as she seems very tired. You'll let me know if there's anything I can do, won't you?' She wanted to ask so much more — if only they would tell her what was actually the matter with Natalie. From the misery on Mark's face, it looked like it was something serious.

He managed the ghost of a smile. 'Thanks, Elsa. I'll see you out.'

The days crawled by. Elsa worked hard, did extra baking, tried to find some enthusiasm for some new summer recipes as it was nearing the end of May. But thoughts of Daniel and the new love they had shared drifted into her mind constantly. And whenever she pushed them out, worry about Natalie found its way in instead.

Feeling the need to expend some energy with vigorous exercise, early on Wednesday morning Elsa looked out her trainers and summer leggings. After tying back her hair into a ponytail, she set off for a run along the prom and down on to the beach. After about an hour, she was pounding back along the sand to the steps up to the promenade when she heard a voice calling her name.

Above her, against the railings she could see the shape of a dark-haired man waving and calling. For a heart-stopping moment as she climbed the steps, she thought it was Daniel — but it couldn't be; he wouldn't be returning from America until the next day.

'Andrew!' She was panting hard with the effort as she reached the top.

Daniel's brother hurried to meet her. 'Elsa, I'm so glad I saw you. I've been knocking on the door of your flat, and was just about to give up.'

Dread suddenly caught her. 'Is something wrong?' Her voice was filled with panic.

'No. I'm sorry if I frightened you.' He began to walk back towards the café with her. 'But it's because of Daniel that I'm here. He told me about what you saw at the ice rink.'

Elsa wiped a hand along the back of her neck, which was damp with cooling sweat. Her legs were heavy with fatigue, and she couldn't reply, as her emotions felt dangerously fragile.

Andrew went on, as she wasn't going to comment. 'He's been desperately worried because you misunderstood what you saw. Irina's mother in Russia has had a heart attack, and she was distraught when she told him. She's taken time off to go to visit her. Daniel was just offering her a compassionate shoulder — and he offered to give her and Dmitri a lift to the airport.'

What he said sounded so plausible.

Suddenly ashamed when she thought about how hard it must be for Irina with a disabled child on her own, Elsa said, 'So he's asked you to come and put his case?' Could she really believe Andrew?

He reached out and took her arm. 'He's talked about nothing else each time I spoke to him this week. He can't concentrate on his business trip for fearing that he's lost you. You must give him the benefit of the doubt, Elsa.'

Elsa searched his face for the truth, wanting to believe these welcome words. 'He's let me down in the past. How can I believe you?'

'Daniel really cares about you, and wants to make this work. I've never seen him as happy as he has been these past few months. You've been really good for him.'

Tears pricked her eyes when she realised how she had been so quick to judge him. 'All right, I promise I'll talk to him properly as soon as he gets back. Tell him to ring me when he's ready.'

She wasn't quite ready to believe everything. After all, it had looked like a very convincing embrace.

Andrew grinned and touched her arm. 'That's the stuff. Can't have you two messing things up again. Anyway, Vicki and I are taking the kids away to Spain for a holiday tomorrow, over the half-term break.'

'I hope you have a great time.' Her thoughts were filled with questions, but it was clear that she needed to speak with Daniel herself.

At that moment, a car drew up beside them. The passenger window wound down electronically, and the driver leaned over. 'Andrew Whitbridge? I'm Nathan Troutbeck, of the *Northern Gazette*. Can I beg a few moments of your time?'

Andrew frowned. 'Why should I talk to you? What about?'

'I want to know why you and your brother haven't brought the police in to investigate at the ice rink when there's clearly something amiss. Your brother always refuses to speak to me.'

'Then you can be assured I won't either. There's nothing to say. Leave us alone,' he said tersely.

Elsa's heart was thumping at this intrusion, all her previous suspicions and fears about Daniel's involvement resurfacing again, though she wouldn't voice them to Andrew. They watched as Troutbeck drove off again, feeling her dislike for the man like a bad taste in her mouth. 'That man's a menace, he's been nosing around for ages,' she told Andrew. 'He even tried to get information from me, under the guise of doing an interview about my business.'

Andrew nodded. 'Don't worry about him. I'll tell Carl, and then Daniel before Vicki and I go off tomorrow.' At that moment his attention was caught by a man on the other side of the road, walking in the direction of the ice rink. 'There's Hank. He'll be on his way to work. I'll walk with him, as I want to talk with Carl today.' He turned to look at her one last time, and she was struck again by his resemblance to Daniel. 'Don't worry, I'm sure you two will work it out together. See you around.'

He ran across the empty road and joined the other man on his way. Elsa suddenly remembered that she had forgotten to ask Andrew about Daniel's car being parked at the ice rink. But before she could call after him, Hank turned and gave Elsa a long look. Startled, she realised that it was the man she had seen with Sean coming from the shop. His gaze somehow looked menacing, and she swivelled on her heel and headed towards the café, feeling disturbed despite the hope that had sparked after hearing Andrew's plea.

A weight seemed to have lifted from her, and the next evening she felt motivated to practise her skating again, as if it could bring her closer to Daniel. If he could really convince her about his innocence, she would apologise unreservedly for her pig-headedness. But he had to be totally honest with her — if he still had any romantic feelings for Irina, then there was no point restarting their relationship. Before leaving the flat she took out the gold acorn and hung the chain round her neck, thinking of Daniel as she fastened the clasp. It seemed to bring him closer to her as it lay against her skin.

As she entered the main door of the rink, she noticed that there was a new young woman with streaked blonde hair in the box office. Elsa's swipe card was short on funds, so she topped up the minimum amount, not keen to add too much in case she didn't want to come very often. As soon as Elsa had taken her card and thanked her, the blonde stepped back from the window and took her mobile phone out of her pocket. Within seconds her head was down, and she was tapping away at the little screen rapidly. Obviously she was the sort of person who was permanently attached to her social media.

It felt good to work her muscles, and Elsa was feeling pleasantly tired from the exercise as she walked home. She was sure that she would sleep better that night. In the twilight she approached the corner of her street, and looked up to the window of the flat. No Missy this time. The cat would want her supper soon. Elsa entered by the door in the side street that led straight upstairs, but as soon as she closed it behind her she knew that something was wrong. There was a breeze blowing along the corridor that went between the café and the back yard.

The back door was ajar. Elsa tried to push it shut, but it wouldn't hold as the lock had been forced. Dread coursed through her as she rushed into the café. 'No, oh no!' she exclaimed at the scene that met her. Tables and chairs were overturned, pictures torn from the walls and crushed on the floor, and the glass of the counter had been smashed. To make matters worse, huge letters in red paint were scrawled across the back wall, spelling the word '*SCUM*'. On shaking legs, she went round the other side of the counter and saw that the till had been rifled. Smashed plates and cups lay on the floor.

Fear gripped her, but she just had to see if the flat had suffered the same treatment. She ran upstairs as fast as she could on her trembling legs. The door had been forced as well, but when she entered only a few drawers had been turned out. Obviously the thieves had been looking for money or valuables. She had little worth taking — her smartphone which she had taken with her was about the most expensive item she owned, and her television was too old to be of any interest. The laptop was locked in a kitchen cupboard.

Her legs would hold her no longer. She sat on the edge of the settee, gulping, trying not to cry. Reaching for the telephone on the table beside it, she stammered out her request for the police. It was only when she disconnected the phone that she realised that there was one supremely important thing missing — Missy.

Adrenaline coursed through her, giving her the strength to leap to her feet, calling for the cat. She looked under the bed, in the cupboards, but there was no sign of her. Then she ran down the stairs and out of the damaged door into the yard, calling all the time. After a while, tears began to run down her cheeks. She hurried back upstairs to find a box of Missy's favourite treats, and came back down to rattle it, calling her name as she did so. But there was no familiar meow, no little grey and white shape streaking towards her. Sobbing, Elsa sat on the bottom stair, hugging the little packet of treats, feeling that her life had reached rock bottom.

It was there that the policewoman found her, and kindly took her back upstairs until she felt strong enough to give a statement. A police forensics officer arrived and processed the crime scene. The policewoman advised Elsa to call a locksmith, and stayed until he had arrived and secured the flat. 'Is there someone you can call, or would you like to go and stay with a relative or friend?'

Elsa thought of Daniel, but he wouldn't have arrived home yet, and in any case they hadn't made up their quarrel. Before he arrived on the scene, it would have been Natalie and Mark who would have been there for her. But that was out of the question at the moment. Plus, her mother wasn't due back from holiday for another week. 'I can't leave the flat — my cat's missing, and I need to be here for her when she comes home.' The thought of losing Missy for ever made her eyes fill with tears.

The policewoman squeezed her arm and left her with a contact number. 'I'll call in tomorrow to see how you're doing. We're finished with forensics, so you can start cleaning up.'

Elsa nodded. It was now well past midnight, so she crept into bed, but only dozed in between shaking. Next day was Saturday, and she was up as soon as it was light, just after half past five. Throwing on some clothes, her first thought was of Missy, so she went down to the yard to rattle the biscuits and call for her. But there was still no sign of her. Heartbroken, she decided to keep busy, and by the time a horrified Lisa reached the door of the café, she had already scraped off the insulting graffiti from the wall, and was sweeping up the debris behind the counter. Their one consolation was that the expensive coffee machine had not been damaged.

The policewoman arrived later, having conducted a door-to-door enquiry, but told Elsa that no one had seen or heard anything. The flat above the electrical shop next door was unoccupied, just used for storage, and the people in the flat beyond had been too far away. The shops looked out to sea, so they were out of the line of sight, and only the fish and chip shop further down would have been open. It would still have been daylight when the attack took place, so even with the blinds down the vandals would have been able to see what they were doing without putting on lights.

They kept the café closed, and Elsa and Lisa spent the few days repainting. During the tidy-up, Elsa came across the dog-eared business card of the reporter, Nathan Troutbeck. Contemplating it for a few minutes, she debated whether to contact him about the break-in, but in the end, undecided, simply tapped his number into her phone contacts and threw the card in the bin. Several times she rang Daniel's phone, telling him she was sorry and they needed to talk. But there was no reply. It seemed that he wasn't wishing to forgive her, after all. Her misery was complete.

Early on the bank holiday Monday, the doorbell to the flat rang. Thinking that it was the glazier coming to measure the counter, she hurried down and threw open the door. To her utter surprise, Natalie stood there, and before Elsa could utter a word, stepped through the doorway and hugged her hard.

# 20

'Mark saw the notice when he passed yesterday. I had to come to find out if you were all right.'

Upstairs in the flat, Elsa wept over her friend, telling her the sorry tale of the vandalism and Missy's disappearance.

'What does Daniel think about this?'

'We — we've split up.' Although she had told her friend at the time, clearly she hadn't taken it in. Elsa described what had happened.

'But he should have been round, no matter what went on between you. That's despicable.'

Elsa shook her head. She just couldn't take everything in. Then she grasped Natalie's hand. 'I've been so worried about you. Please, tell me what's wrong.'

Natalie took a deep breath. 'I've just

been rather overwhelmed. I was feeling so lousy when we got back from holiday, and when the doctor suggested that I might be pregnant, I laughed. But soon I wasn't laughing — it's true, I'm four months gone.' She shrugged ruefully. 'You know me, I never wanted to have kids. Just Mark and me. The thought of bringing a baby into the world, being a mother ... I just couldn't visualise it. To make matters worse, I was plagued by the most horrendous pregnancy sickness, not just in the morning, but *all the time*. That's why they took me into hospital.'

'Oh, Natalie.' Elsa stroked her arm. 'I thought that you were dying and couldn't tell me.'

Natalie laughed through her tears. 'It seemed almost worse than that at the time — I had to take a decision whether to go ahead with the pregnancy. In the end I looked at Mark and realised what a great dad he would be. Plus, I began to feel better, and came to the conclusion that it was just a massive surge in hormones that was making me feel so negative. I began to feel more in control towards the end of last week, and you know, I'm actually beginning to feel excited about a new adventure, even though it won't be easy.'

They embraced again. 'Well, I'll be delighted to be an honorary auntie.' At that moment the telephone rang. Elsa answered it quickly, and her face broke into a smile. 'What? Oh, yes, yes, I'll be there immediately. Thank you, thank you so much.'

Incredulously she looked at Natalie. 'It's Missy — the vet has her. Someone brought her in yesterday. She was hiding in their garden, and has a cut on her paw. But she's going to be fine. They found me through her microchip.'

'Oh, thank goodness.'

The next day, feeling much happier now that the café was up and running again, Natalie was close to her once more and Missy was home, Elsa began to wonder about the motivation for the break-in. Some part of her suspected that there was a connection with the ice rink. It was a bitter blow that Daniel hadn't contacted her since coming back from America. His silence puzzled her, as all the calls and texts that he had sent before he went, plus Andrew's message, implied that he did truly want to work things out. She understood that he would have been busy since coming back, but she really needed his input on the break-in.

By the next day Elsa had rung his flat several times, and left more messages and texts on his mobile, but there was still no reply. Could he still be in America? She didn't want to ask anyone at the ice rink, because she didn't want to explain their break up to anyone else. Instead, she decided to take the bus over to his flat during the evening to see if she could speak to him face to face.

Daniel lived in a village on the outskirts of the city, but it meant taking a bus into the city centre, and a second one out to the village. He liked living outside the city, so he had jumped at the chance of renting this upper flat in a row of old terraced houses. The main door was at the side, where a lane led round the back to a parking area for the residents. After ringing the doorbell several times and trying his home phone and mobile once more, she was still met with silence. However, a quick reconnoitre told her that his car wasn't round the back. Maybe he was just out. By a lucky chance, his downstairs neighbour drove in at that moment. Elsa asked him if he had seen Daniel in the past few days.

The older man shook his head. 'I thought I saw him a few days ago, but I haven't notice him around since. I haven't heard any movement in the flat, either, like I usually do when he's at home.'

Despondent and worried now, Elsa realised that she had done all she could. She retraced her steps, though she had half an hour to wait for the next bus. It was after ten o'clock when she caught the bus from the city centre, and getting on towards eleven when she stepped off at the bus stop near the ice rink. As she neared her flat, a huge lorry roared past and headed for the ice rink. Elsa took a few more paces, then stopped. Could this be the key to the mystery? Curious, she decided to head down in that direction. There was little traffic now.

The huge black shape of the rink dominated the dark skyline. The car park was empty, so there mustn't be any late night ice training going on. Taking a deep breath, she decided to take a look round the back. She was wearing navy jeans and a black jacket, so she wouldn't be very visible. As she neared the corner of the rink, she could hear low voices and the sound of the rear platform of the truck being lowered. Peeking round tentatively, she saw that the back door was open. Two men disappeared inside.

Taking refuge out of sight, she took her phone from her pocket, glad that something had prompted her to put

Nathan Troutbeck's number in her contacts. To her relief, he answered almost immediately.

'Nathan, it's Elsa Turnfield. One of those lorries is at the ice rink now, and I think they're going to load something. I'm going inside — and Daniel's missing. I don't know if there's a connection.'

'Wait, I'll call the police. Don't go in alone.'

'I won't let them see me. I know my way round.'

'Elsa . . . '

She disconnected and switched the phone to silent, tucking it in her jeans pocket. The men hadn't reappeared as she edged her way up to the door while listening acutely for any sounds inside. There was nothing. She risked looking round the door, and slipped inside. She was in the back corridor, well beyond the cafeteria area. The farthest door to the ice surface was just ahead of her. Luckily it was never locked, for she had to duck quickly through the swing

330

doors as she heard voices and footsteps approaching. The icy air enveloped her, but she hardly heeded it as her heart was pounding.

Crouching so that only one eye was above the window area, she could see three men carrying boxes. As they neared her, the smallest one tripped and his box went flying, bursting open on the floor. Elsa almost gasped as she saw a cascade of cigarette boxes flow out. It must be a smuggling operation! There were angry curses from the other two men. The small fellow stood up and she recognised Sean, Pete and Gina's grandson. He looked cowed. No doubt these were the bad element that he had got in with, but he didn't look at all happy.

Elsa made her way through the seats to the next door. The ice area was eerie and quiet, a vast, chilly expanse, dimly lit by only a few safety lights. A mist hung over the dark ice, like a ghostly emanation. The cold began to seep through her clothing.

From the next door she was looking out on to the skate hire area. Some of the box benches were upturned, and were lined with cardboard cartons like those which the men had been carrying. There were many benches round the area, so there was room for a lot of cigarettes. No wonder the police hadn't found anything. No one would think of looking inside the benches. Pete must have been involved somehow, because he had been very jittery when Elsa found that piece missing a few weeks back.

Looking warily through the glass, she could see no one. She edged through the door and hurried across to the stairs to the upper rooms. The stairs were dark, but slivers of light came through from the safety lights. A quick survey of the upper rooms proved them to be empty, and the rink managers' office was locked. She spoke Daniel's name softly at the door, but there was no response. Returning downstairs, she heard the men coming back for another load. Once they had gone, she tiptoed into the corridor and began checking the maintenance rooms, opening and closing the doors gently. Those that were locked, she tapped on gently, whispering 'Daniel?' as loud as she dared. But there was nothing. Eventually she reached the dark box office, beyond which were the dressing rooms.

Elsa chose the smaller dressing room first, putting her ear to the door. Her heart began to pound as she heard a muffled sound inside. Only hesitating a moment, she moved the door open slowly. There was a lamp on in the room. It took a few moments for her to discern Daniel and Pete, gagged and bound on chairs at the far end.

Elsa rushed forward. Daniel shook his head from side to side, struggling to be free of his gag. She pulled it down.

'Elsa, what are you doing? You don't know what you're risking, coming in here!' He looked pale and haggard, with a few days' growth of beard on his face.

'Just tell me how I can get you free. Is

there anything I can use to cut your bonds?'

'The box office should be open, and there are usually a few pairs of ice skates waiting to be collected after sharpening. Take care!' His voice was anxious.

Luckily the box office door was unlocked, so she grabbed two pairs of skates, choosing the smallest ones as she thought that they would be less cumbersome to use. Back in the changing rooms, she carefully angled the sharp blade and began chafing at the rope that bound Daniel's wrists. Her breathing was hoarse with fear as she tried to avoid cutting his flesh. Newly ground ice skate blades were lethally sharp.

At last the bonds separated, and Daniel grabbed another skate to work on the rope tying his ankles to the chair. 'Help Pete, now.'

The elderly man looked at her with anguish in his eyes as she slipped off his gag. 'You shouldn't be doing this, lass.

These men are dangerous.'

'Not Sean, surely,' she said as she began working on the ropes.

Pete's voice was sad. 'I'm afraid that one of the other lads got him into this, just asked him if he wanted to earn some extra cash. Naturally the lad agreed, and found he was doing a lot of their dirty work — including the damage at your café. He came to me in tears afterwards. I wanted to inform the police, but that other lad heard me and jumped me when I was coming out from work last night. He told me that they had threatened my Gina if she said anything. Ouch!' he exclaimed as the bonds came away, and he began rubbing his wrists. 'I knew there was something going on, as they were asking me to do jobs and not let on to the management.'

'Like the seats in the skate hire area.'

He nodded grimly. 'Aye, lass. I knew you were looking at me funny that day, and had to warn you off.'

Daniel had managed to free one

ankle. 'They took me three days ago. I was on my way to see you, and saw one of their vehicles entering the rink, where I stumbled across them unloading. They've been keeping me in the storeroom at the far end, as it's never used, but I've been moved around a few times. I don't know what they were planning to do to me once this shipment was away.'

At that moment the door burst open, and Robert Fitzsimmons hurtled through. He grabbed the ice skate from Daniel's hand. 'Drop it!' he barked at Elsa, who let the skate fall from her hands, seeing that he was holding the sharp skate blade against Daniel's throat. Shaking with fear, she stood behind Pete's chair, watching Robert warily.

'I should just cut your throat and be done with it,' he snarled. 'You've caused enough trouble round here — you were never wanted.' The blade had already nicked Daniel's neck, and blood was trickling down on to his sweatshirt. Elsa could see his muscles bunching in his arms, and realised that he was about to resist, but she frowned at him, willing him not to fight back. That blade was just too close.

'I presume it was you who put the pills in your father's drink that night,' Daniel said through clenched teeth.

'Shut up!' The blade edged nearer. 'You have no idea what it was like, trying to convince that stubborn old man not to let the ice rink go. He'd forked out some money to cover me when I got in a bit deep with my debts, but wouldn't cough up any more. This place is worth a pretty penny — it would have been easy to take out a loan on it. But he refused. One big win was all I needed, and I could get that once I had my hands on it. But Carl brought you in anyway.' He swore angrily. 'So when I heard that there was someone looking for somewhere to stash smuggled cigarettes after they were landed nearby, I jumped at the chance. It was ideal

— except for all you nosey people!'

'Gambling always was your downfall, Robert. But you didn't have to involve my grandson.' Pete's voice was weary.

'Stuff it, old man. Sean!' Robert yelled. 'Go and get some more rope! We've got three prisoners now.'

A minute later, the door opened again — but it wasn't Sean. It was a policeman wearing a black combat vest. 'Your lot have all been arrested, and they're spilling the beans, so I shouldn't try anything if I were you.'

Robert's eyes bulged with fury, and his hand convulsed. Then he flung away the skate, putting his hands behind his neck and lowering his head in defeat. Another policeman burst into the room and quickly pulled Robert's hands behind his waist to cuff them. Once they had gone, Elsa rushed over to tend to Daniel, but looked up as Nathan entered. He gave a grin. 'Not such a far-fetched idea after all, was it?'

All her antipathy towards him melting away, Elsa nodded her head.

'Thanks, Nathan. You saved us.' Seeing Daniel's inquisitive expression, she explained about the journalist's suspicions, and how she had kept his number. 'I was furious with him, but it turned out he was right.'

'But not about me!' Daniel pulled away the last of his ankle bond and stood up gingerly, waiting for the feeling to come back into his feet. The first policeman had produced a knife to cut Pete's remaining bonds, and was helping him stand up. The officer insisted on taking them all to the hospital for a check-up, though Elsa explained that she hadn't been a prisoner.

Several hours later, when Daniel emerged from the ward, his eyes widened when he noticed Elsa waiting for him. 'I thought you'd be long gone. It's very late.'

'I wanted to make sure that you were OK.' The shock and terror of the past few hours, as well as all the emotions that had assailed her in the past weeks, were near the surface, making her voice tremble. She just wanted to throw herself into his arms, but held back, not knowing what he was feeling.

He touched the dressing on his neck. 'I am — thanks to you. If you hadn't contacted Nathan, I don't know what would have happened.'

She pushed her hands into her pockets and walked with him along the corridor. 'I don't know — maybe Robert wouldn't have become violent if I hadn't turned up.'

'It's hard to tell if someone's a killer. Though he must have been pretty desperate to do what he did to his father. His gambling debts must have been huge. I hope Carl will still want to continue in partnership with me — I've always liked him, and believe he had nothing to do with all this. I'm just glad we're all safe.'

'What will happen to Sean?'

'He'll need to face charges, naturally, but the poor lad was living in fear, so I hope that they'll give him a chance.

He's been a good worker.'

Although she was desperate to bring up the reasons for their parting, she wanted him to speak first. But one other mystery needed clearing up. 'Daniel — why was your car at the ice rink while you were away?'

He gave a short laugh. 'I let my brother borrow it for a few days as Vicki wanted to use their own car for some other activities. I suppose you began to imagine all sorts.'

'It did throw me, I must admit.'

'When I called in at the ice rink that night, I didn't want to attract attention, so I parked in one of the side streets nearby. I hope the car's still there.'

They emerged into the night air. 'Can I borrow your phone to call us a taxi? They took my phone off me when I was locked up.'

He directed the taxi to pick them up outside the hospital gates, and they began to walk away from the activity around the entrance. Elsa felt treacherous tears close to the surface, but as they reached the gate, his arm came round her shoulders.

'Elsa, I know this isn't the ideal place to talk about what happened with us.' They stopped, and he took her hands in his. 'I want to apologise for exposing you to this danger, and for hurting you. I've suspected for a long time that there was something illegal going on at the rink, and I was trying to protect you by keeping you at a distance. I'm so sorry I missed your presentation — I know it meant a lot to you, and I should have been there with you. I could have ducked out of the meeting, but I thought it would be a good opportunity to talk with Carl about my suspicions before going to America. As it turned out, he called off! Then Irina arrived to tell me about her mother, and I knew that she needed a friend to take her to the airport that night.'

Elsa felt ashamed again at how she had behaved. 'Andrew told me about that. I wish I'd let you explain.'

He shook his head and continued, 'It

was only when I was so far away without you that I realised how empty my life would be without you. I was longing to come home and explain everything, but then I ended up in that mess at the ice rink.' Gently he touched the gold acorn at her neck with one finger. 'All I could think about when I was tied up was that you're the woman that I love dearly and want to spend the rest of my life with. I should never have let you go all those years ago.'

The ice round Elsa's heart was rapidly melting as she came closer to him, slipping her arms round his waist and resting her head on his chest. 'Oh, Daniel, I've missed you so much. I'm sorry for being so pig-headed, and not trusting you. Of course Irina and Dmitri needed your help, and I quite understand. I've a lot to tell you — about Natalie, about the café, and about Missy — but at last I feel that we can be our true selves with each other. I love you too, and I would love to skate into the future with you.' Their bodies felt so right together as she leaned into him. Every part of her felt alive, her senses heightened.

'Good,' he murmured, and lowered his head to kiss her deeply. She responded with a hungry passion, as if she had been starved of him over the past weeks. When they finally surfaced, he smiled, gazing deep into her eyes. 'Partners in life, and on ice — I'm going to take you to Sun City for our honeymoon to skate on that outdoor rink. We won't fall on the ice when we have each other.'